Lilah's

I made out with a stranger last night. Yes, me, the girl who wears rubber gloves to carry trash cans to the curb, had my lips and tongue completely interlocked with a man I barely know. It's true, I've been in New York one day, and I've already succumbed to the debauchery. I wasn't fazed by the white-knuckle flight, the cab driver with a death wish or the cranky bouncer. But put me in a crowded room with a bed that sleeps sixteen and a hot guy, and I completely lose my cool. But before you book me a ticket on the next train to Skankytown, let me explain....

ROBYN AMOS

After graduating from college with a degree in psychology, Robyn Amos worked a multitude of day jobs while pursuing a career in writing. After marrying her real-life romantic hero, a genuine rocket scientist, she was finally able to live her dream of writing full-time. Since her first book was published in 1997, Robyn has written tales of romantic comedy and suspense for several publishers, including Kensington, Harlequin and HarperCollins. A native of the Washington, D.C. metropolitan area, Robyn currently resides in Odenton, Maryland.

Lilah's LIST

Robyn Amos

KIMANI™ ROMANCE

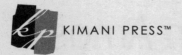

KIMANI PRESS™

ISBN-13: 978-0-373-86049-4
ISBN-10:   0-373-86049-8

LILAH'S LIST

Copyright © 2008 by Robyn Amos

www.kimanipress.com

Printed in U.S.A.

Dear Reader,

I had so much fun working on *Lilah's List*. Taking the point of view of a young woman trying to cram in as many life experiences as she can before turning thirty required some unique research. And it also helped me realize that, although I'm a bit past thirty myself, there are many life experiences I would still like to have.

In honor of *Lilah's List*, I ice-skated at Rockefeller Center and visited the Statue of Liberty. I ate at some amazing New York restaurants and even dined on a bed in the nightclub where Lilah and Tyler meet. I didn't have the nerve or the inclination to do some of Lilah's more outrageous tasks, such as get a tattoo or crash a party. But, thanks to my new perspective of write it down and make it happen, I planned my first trip to Europe so I could see Paris, and I'm still in search of a mechanical bull that I can ride.

I hope you enjoy Lilah's journey to find herself, which eventually leads her to find her soul mate—even though she'd already crossed falling in love off her list.

I love to hear from readers. E-mail me at robynamos@aol.com or visit me on the Web at www.robynamos.com.

Happy reading,

Robyn Amos

Lilah's List is for my dear friends Judy Fitzwater and Pat Gagne, and my husband, John Pope. Without them, I never would have gotten through this book.

Lilah's List

1. Date Reggie Martin
2. ~~Read all the works of Shakespeare~~
3. ~~Learn French~~
4. ~~Watch *Casablanca, Gone with the Wind* and *Citizen Kane*~~
5. ~~Ride in a hot-air balloon~~
6. ~~Learn to play the guitar~~
7. ~~Learn karate~~
8. Shake hands with someone famous
9. ~~Fall in love~~
10. ~~Learn how to drive a stick shift~~
11. ~~Make up a new word and use it in a conversation~~
12. Get a professional makeover
13. Learn to knit
14. ~~Visit Paris~~
15. ~~Swim with dolphins~~
16. Sing at a karaoke bar
17. ~~Learn to rap~~
18. ~~Write a love letter~~
19. Eat escargot
20. ~~See an active volcano~~
21. Visit a fortune-teller
22. ~~Talk a cop out of a ticket~~
23. ~~Go to Mardi Gras in New Orleans~~
24. ~~Visit a nude beach~~

25. Ride a mechanical bull
26. Throw a wild party
27. Get a tattoo
28. Kiss a stranger
29. Ride a motorcycle
30. Crash a party
31. Do something scandalous
32. Protest for a worthy cause
33. Leave a $100 tip
34. ~~Learn sign language~~
35. Practice a random act of kindness
36. ~~Go skinny-dipping~~
37. ~~Learn kickboxing~~
38. Have multiple orgasms
39. ~~Learn to dance the tango~~
40. ~~Get real estate license~~
41. Have 15 minutes of fame
42. Go out in public with no underwear
43. Fly first-class
44. Buy something without reading the price tag
45. Spend an entire day in bed
46. Own an expensive designer dress
47. Drink Cristal champagne straight from the bottle
48. ~~Go to Hawaii~~
49. Climb to the top of the Statue of Liberty
50. Ice skate at Rockefeller Center

Chapter 1

Multiple orgasms were among the many things she wasn't going to get to experience before turning thirty, Lilah Banks decided as she stared at her well-worn pink stationery. She hadn't seen her list since college graduation in 1999.

That day she'd crossed off *fall in love* and neatly tucked The List inside her grandmother's antique jewelry box. The jewelry box had been packed up along with her other college memories and had landed in the attic of the house she'd shared with her husband Chuck.

Until today, that box had remained sealed like Pandora's box. When Lilah had opened it, all of her unfulfilled hopes and dreams had tumbled out with her American University sweatshirt and a ton of old photos.

Lilah had been a good girl and followed the rules. She'd married her college sweetheart, lost her virginity on her wedding night and perfectly balanced her career in real estate with her duties as a domestic goddess. Yet here she was divorced after only six years of marriage.

She smoothed her hand over The List, studying the handwriting of a sixteen-year-old girl as it transformed into that of a young woman in her twenties.

At sixteen she'd wanted to date Reggie Martin—never happened. At eighteen, rebelling against her goody-two-shoes image, she added *visit a nude beach* to The List—that did happen: spring break 1997. At twenty, the awakening of her social consciousness, she'd wanted to protest a worthy cause—but never did. And at twenty-one, the awakening of her sexual consciousness, came the thing about multiple orgasms.

Lilah shook her head. A lot of really *fun* things were still unchecked, and her thirtieth birthday was only three weeks away.

"So much for that." She dropped The List to the floor and dug back into the box. She pulled out a framed photo of her kissing Chuck at the Kappa Alpha Psi fraternity cookout senior year.

Saving the frame, she tossed the photo into the waste bin at her right. Her world had been so different then.

At this point in her life she'd expected to be preparing for motherhood instead of readjusting to single life. She should have been remodeling their fabulous three-story suburban home instead of unpacking her Georgetown condo after three months of living out of boxes.

The only part of her life that had stayed on track was her career. As a real estate agent she was at the top of her game, making more money than she knew how to spend. But, with her personal life so deep in the trash bin, it was hard to celebrate that success.

She plunged both hands into the box and pulled out the last picture frame. Lilah and her best friend Angie. They were lying on their dorm room floor, staring up into the camera she'd held above their heads. When the two of them were together, they were trouble. Their parents had nicknamed them Lucy and Ethel because of their madcap adventures.

Angie was still Lilah's best friend, but they'd grown apart since college, and Lilah's marriage had had a lot to do with that.

After college Angie had moved to New York City to pursue her career as the next big name in fashion. Lilah had been certain she'd be spending a lot of time in the Big Apple visiting Angie, and had added a couple of New York-related items to her list. But, over the years, Chuck had always found reasons for Lilah not to make the trip.

Lilah bit back her rising anger over all the times she'd given in to Chuck's emotional manipulations. He'd been needy and insecure, and she'd been spineless and desperate to please. What a pair they'd made.

Her gaze dropped back to the two girls in the picture. Feeling a surge of wistfulness, Lilah grabbed her phone and began to dial. It was ten-thirty on a Saturday night, so the odds were strongly against her friend answering, but it had already been too long since they'd last spoken.

"Hello?"

"Angie, I'm so glad you're there."

"Lilah?" croaked a weaker version of Angie's vibrant timbre.

"Did I catch you at a bad time? You sound exhausted."

"It's never a bad time to talk to you, but I *was* running around the city all day looking for platinum buttons. Not gold. Not silver. Platinum—for some diva who doesn't let any lesser metals touch her skin."

While she was awaiting her big break, Angie was sewing costumes for an off-Broadway playhouse.

"Aw, honey, I'm sorry to hear you had such a rough day."

"Don't worry, as it turns out, Miss Thing doesn't know the difference between silver and platinum after all."

Lilah laughed. "You're so bad."

"That's why you love me."

"Anyway, I was finally unpacking the last of my boxes today, and you'll never believe what I found."

"Um, two million dollars' worth of gold bullion that you're looking to split with your best friend?"

"I found *The List*."

"The List? Fifty things you wanted to do before thirty? Hey, your thirtieth birthday is next month. How far did you get?"

Lilah scanned the sheet, mentally crossing off a couple of things she'd accomplished in the last eight years. "I guess I'm almost halfway through it."

"November tenth is—" She paused for calculation. "Twenty-one days away. Are you going to try to finish it off?"

Lilah huffed. "Some of these things aren't even possible anymore. Remember item number one—date Reggie Martin?"

Angie sighed. "Well, that one's not impossible. Just a bit of a challenge."

"Ha! Have you listened to your radio lately? Reggie Martin is even more unattainable now than when he was just your average high school stud."

Reggie Martin was the sole reason Lilah had made The List in the first place. Her father had been giving her some sort of pep talk about how anything was possible if she identified her goals and worked toward them. Sure, he'd been referring to things like college and career, but at the time, Lilah had been obsessed with Reggie Martin.

It had taken a great deal of self-restraint not to write *marry Reggie Martin* at the top of The List, but she'd decided to stay within the realm of possibility. He was the lean-muscled, baby-faced, track-running, future superstar that she'd tutored in math.

"I don't know," Angie argued. "I think we got you pretty close in high school. I had to bake Bobby Carnivelli cookies for two months so he'd let you take over as Reggie's math tutor. It's not my fault you were too shy to make the first move."

For her entire junior and senior year, she and Angie had devised many a plot to get Reggie's attention, all of which stopped just short of her confessing her undying love. A girl had to have her pride.

"I'm old-fashioned. I prefer the gentleman to do the asking."

"Old-fashioned, my gluteus maximus. You were just a big, fat chicken."

"Oh ho. Was I chicken in the sixth grade when I talked LaTonya Richards out of beating you up?"

"Well—"

"And what about the time I convinced a Maryland State Trooper not to give you yet another ticket. The ticket that would have ultimately caused you to lose your license. And—"

"I meant with boys, okay? You're a big, fat chicken when it comes to boys."

"Fine. I'll concede on that point. Which brings us back to the issue at hand. Number one on my list, date Reggie Martin, has gone from unlikely to impossible. He's a superstar now."

Reggie had always been a singer. He had a lovely melodic voice and could be found singing on almost any occasion. But no one could have predicted that he'd manage to parlay that into a career. Right now, his first single, "Love Triangle," was getting heavy rotation on all the air waves.

"He's not a superstar yet—more like a rising star. It's not the same as trying to get a date with somebody like…Usher." Angie was eternally optimistic, which was one of the qualities Lilah missed most about her.

"Yeah, whatever, girl. Keep hitting that crack pipe."

"Okay, put number one aside for now. What else is left on your list?"

"Eat escargot, ride a mechanical bull, get a tattoo, crash a party—"

"Slow down there, girlfriend. Those are all things you can still do."

"Angie, I don't even *want* a tattoo."

"That point is moot. Listen…. I have a plan—"

In the past those four words between them would have given her a charge, but Lilah's mature, twenty-nine-year-old self had learned to avoid trouble at all costs. "No, *I* have a plan. How about we forget I ever mentioned the stupid list and talk about something else."

"Not a chance. Here's what I think—you should come to New York a week before your birthday, and we'll knock The List out."

"Remember number one—"

"I said I have a plan."

"You have a plan to get me a date with the hottest new R&B singer?"

"No, I have a plan to get you a date with an old, high school friend who *happens* to be a hot new R&B singer."

"Okay, let's hear it. This ought to be good."

"As I see it, we have two viable avenues by which to reach Reggie. One, I read that his older brother Tyler is his business manager, and he lives here in the city. We can try to contact him and enlist his help hooking up with Reggie."

Lilah remembered Reggie's older brother well. And she'd always been a tiny bit scared of him. If Reggie were sunshine, Tyler was a thunder cloud—a dark, brooding killjoy. During her tutoring sessions, Reggie had complained rather frequently about how hard his brother rode him. She'd always suspected Tyler was jealous of Reggie's talent and popularity.

"And the second avenue?"

"Well, you can't live in New York and work in the fashion industry without being hot-wired into the celebrity grapevine. With his brother managing his business affairs here in the city, odds are he either lives here or frequents the area. I know my contacts can dig up the dirt on his whereabouts. Then it's just a matter of matching the two of you up in time and space."

Sure, it sounded straightforward, even plausible, but Lilah knew from experience that their schemes never went according to plan. "Well, I have to hand it to you, Ang, that's not bad. You certainly haven't lost your touch."

"So we're on?"

"Not. A. Chance."

"What? Why not?"

"I have to work."

"I know for a fact you haven't taken any time off since the divorce. That was a year and a half ago. You must have vacation accrued up to your eyeballs."

"I just moved. There's still so much to be done around here."

"Nothing that can't wait."

"It's just not a good time…."

Angie was silent for a minute. "Wow, I guess your marriage really did crush all the life out of you. You've lost your sense of adventure."

Lilah gasped. That was a low blow. And it hit its mark. She'd been a good girl. She'd played by the rules. It hadn't made her happy.

She couldn't remember the last time she'd been utterly content. Her wedding day? College? She'd gotten so used to the status quo that she didn't even challenge herself anymore.

Her gaze fell back on The List. Maybe she needed to practice a random act of kindness. Maybe she *needed* to drink champagne straight from the bottle. She definitely needed to climb to the top of the Statue of Liberty and ice skate in Rockefeller Center. She'd promised her best friend that they'd do those things together.

"Okay, I'm in."

Over the next week Angie and Lilah talked nearly every day working out the arrangements for her visit. Lilah ended up taking off the entire two weeks before her birthday. After all, she was overdue for a vacation, and she'd need all the time she could get to work her way through The List. She'd booked a first-class flight—scratch that off The List—from D.C. to New York Friday morning.

Angie tapped into the grapevine and discovered that Reggie did, in fact, live in Manhattan. According to Reggie's bass player's wife's hairdresser, he was attending a private party in the Flatiron District Friday night.

"The party's at some trendy club called Duvet," Angie informed her the night before. "I ran a Google search and apparently they serve you food and cocktails on these enormous cushion-lined beds."

"Let's see—private party, Friday night, trendy club. Sounds like it'll be hard to get into. We could be waiting outside in the cold for hours—if they let us in at all."

"Oh, we'll get in. We have to."

"And why is that?"

"Because *crash a party* is on your list."

Chapter 2

Lilah's List Blog Entry
October 27, 2007

I made out with a stranger last night. Yes, me, the girl who wears rubber gloves to carry trash cans to the curb, had my lips and tongue completely interlocked with a man I barely know. It's true, I've been in New York one day, and I've already succumbed to the debauchery. I wasn't fazed by the white-knuckle flight, the cab driver with a death wish or the cranky Jamaican bouncer. But put me in a crowded room with a bed that sleeps sixteen and a hot guy, and I completely lose my cool. But before you book me a ticket on the next train to Skankytown, let me explain.

When she'd boarded the plane for New York that morning, Lilah had felt daring. Her blood had pumped with excitement. Whether or not she returned with a tattoo, a designer dress or a date with a celebrity didn't matter. For two weeks she was going to have fun, spend some much-needed time with her best friend, and live on the edge.

She'd headed for her first-class window seat only to find a gentleman already occupying it. Eventually the stewardess was able to sort out the mixup, but that didn't keep Lilah from feeling conspicuously like a fraud.

To make matters worse, the plane sat on the tarmac for forty-five minutes while some unexplained mechanical trouble was investigated. Thank goodness the flight was only an hour long, because Lilah white-knuckled it the entire way. So much for first-class—it was lost in a blur of fear and mimosas.

After struggling with her bags and arguing with the taxi driver for trying to make a daring pass into oncoming traffic that had nearly killed them, Lilah finally arrived at the Casablanca Hotel. It was a self-proclaimed oasis in the heart of Times Square. She chose the place because *Casablanca* was one of her favorite movies. And watching it was one of the first things she was able to cross off The List.

She'd had romantic fantasies of sitting in front of the fireplace in Rick's Café and listening to "As Time Goes By" on her iPod. Unfortunately she didn't even take the time to soak in the vibrantly colored Moroccan decor. Instead she flopped down on the king-size bed and slept like the dead all afternoon.

Lilah was just returning to a groggy consciousness when Angie began pounding on her door early that evening. "Take it easy," Lilah said, opening the door, heedless of her nap-mussed hair and wrinkled T-shirt and jeans.

Angie stood in the doorway, hand on hip, as she looked Lilah up and down. She clicked her tongue. "It's just as I suspected. So much to do and so little time."

Lilah blinked at her friend. "I love you, too."

Then she was swept off her feet as the taller woman lifted her into a bear hug. "I'm so happy you're finally here. We're going to have so much fun."

Angie reached into the hallway for the suitcase she'd brought along, and bounded into the room, filling it with her energy. But Lilah was feeling the opposite of energetic. Her days of staying up late and going out were long in her past. If the truth were told, she could get much more excited about room service and a movie rental than the agenda Angie was laying out for them.

"We have to get to Duvet early, otherwise we'll never get past the door. But don't worry, I have a fool-proof plan to get us in."

"Great," Lilah said, falling back on the tousled bed sheets.

"Have you been sleeping all day?" It was an accusation.

"Yup," she answered without remorse. "I could barely sleep last night thinking about this trip. You know, the more I think about The List, the more impossible it seems."

Angie stopped rummaging through the closet to stare at her. "Since when do we let the impossible stand in our way? Two days before senior prom, when we were doomed to being *each other's* dates, it was your idea to storm the University of Maryland campus and ask every cute guy we saw to the prom. You had every girl at Richard Montgomery High School wondering how two nobodies scored dates with hot college boys."

"Yeah," Lilah said absently.

"You used to be fearless, remember? You could talk anyone into anything. What happened to you?"

When Lilah looked back on some of the stunts

she and Angie had pulled in their youth, it blew her mind. She couldn't imagine approaching situations with the same reckless abandon she'd once had.

Lilah looked at Angie and shrugged. "What happened to me? I grew up."

After a few moments of awkward silence, Angie turned her attention back to Lilah's closet and began throwing her clothes around the room.

"None of these clothes are acceptable for tonight's activities, and there's no time for shopping." Angie walked over to her suitcase and opened it up. "Fortunately for you, I came prepared. It's an original creation and it will look stunning on you."

It was a burnt-orange swirly-print cocktail dress with a complicated weaving of spaghetti straps across the back. It stopped just above Lilah's knees with dainty flair. Lilah studied herself in the mirror. The dress was beautiful, if a bit bold for her taste.

"Good Lord, are those the only shoes you have?" Angie turned up her nose at Lilah's functional, decidedly nondesigner black pumps.

"I'm afraid so, unless you think my pink Timberlands would work with this look."

"I guess the pumps are going to have to do. I don't know how you balance on those tiny pinpricks you call feet, anyway," she said with a comical glare that had the two of them bursting into giggles. Angie's feet were two sizes bigger than Lilah's—and Angie all but hated her for it.

Lilah piled her light brown hair atop her head in one of those sloppy knots she'd seen in magazines. She was going for an air of elegant maturity. She silently prayed she didn't look the way she felt—like a little girl playing dress-up.

Physically, Lilah hadn't changed much since high school. She still got carded on a regular basis. With her clear champagne complexion, no makeup and her honey-brown hair worn loose, she was a dead ringer for sixteen.

It would be a few more years before Lilah felt being mistaken for someone younger could actually be flattering instead of mildly annoying. Her tiny, soft voice did nothing to help matters. That was why Lilah relied on makeup and a severe topknot to force clients to take her seriously. She also tried as hard as possible not to be bubbly.

Angie, on the other hand, epitomized bubbly. Add that to her two-toned Macy Gray fro and funky homemade clothes, and people frequently underestimated her wickedly keen mind.

Angie in her typical statement-making fashion, was wearing a skintight vinyl tube that passed as a dress. With this she wore black leggings and multicolored paint-splattered boots, under a long dark coat straight from *The Matrix*. With her orange curling Afro frosted at the tips, her hair radiated from her head like rays of sunshine.

"Okay, are you ready to hear my strategy?" Angie asked later as they rode to the Flatiron District in a taxi. The late October night air had just enough bite for them to need overcoats, but it wasn't cold enough for gloves and scarves yet.

"I can't wait," Lilah answered, deflated. She wasn't looking forward to this adventure. In fact, considering the way her trip had begun, she was convinced this entire outing would be a disaster.

"Listen up, I have a three-tiered plan to get us past the doorman. Phase one, and the least likely to work, we flash our brilliant smiles and sweetly ask to be let in."

"If that's unlikely to work, Angie, why is it even part of the plan?"

"Because we're attractive women—we're armed with mother nature's tools. It never hurts to try them out."

Lilah rolled her eyes. "What's phase two?"

"We drop the high school connection."

"What?"

"We tell the bouncer we went to high school with Reggie Martin."

That gave Lilah a start. She hadn't seen Reggie since high school graduation. Would he even remember her?

She took a deep breath. Of course he would. She'd spent countless hours in his house for their tutoring sessions. He usually turned up an hour or so after she did, which gave her plenty of time to take in personal details and talk to his family about him.

And he'd been so nice to her. He always made sure she had a ride home with his brother whenever he couldn't take her himself. He would even confide in her about his family problems.

But what would she say to him after all these years? Suddenly The List sounded so juvenile. Hopefully, he wouldn't laugh in her face.

"Please tell me phase three is a real winner. Otherwise I suggest we turn this cab around and go have a nice dinner. I haven't eaten all day."

"Phase three is a sure thing."

"I'm listening."

"Filet mignon."

"You agree we should go for dinner?"

"No, that's the code word."

"What are you talking about?"

"Apparently all bouncers know this code word. It means let us in immediately, we're very important people."

"And just where did you get this information?"

She pointed out the window. "Look, we're almost there."

"No changing the subject. Where did you hear this?"

Angie sighed. "The Internet."

Lilah's spine snapped straight. "Driver!"

Angie grabbed her arm and covered Lilah's mouth. "Shh. This is going to work. You'll see."

Lilah climbed out of the cab, her legs trembling ever so slightly. "This is going to be so humiliating."

Angie gripped her elbow and started marching her forward. "You know the drill. Say everything with confidence and authority, and you'll have those bouncers eating out of your hand."

They approached a tall, dark-skinned man with dreadlocks and a black leather trench coat. "Hi, we're here for the party," Angie said brightly.

The man frowned at her. "We don't open to the public until after midnight tonight. We have a private party going on," he answered with a thick Jamaican accent.

"That's right," Angie continued. "We're here for the party."

The man just shook his head.

"We're meeting our high school friend Reggie here. *Reggie Martin.*"

The man pointed over Angie's shoulder to the long line stretching down the block.

"What's that line for?"

"Dat's for everyone who wants to be let in after midnight."

"But it's only eight-thirty."

His gaze remained cold.

"By the way," Angie said finally. "We're filet mignon."

The bouncer glared at her. "Really, 'cuz you look more like chopped liver." He turned to Lilah. "And this one barely looks over eighteen. Don't try flashing dem fake IDs 'round here. I can spot 'em a mile away."

"Now wait a minute," Lilah said, finally finding her voice. "There's no need to be rude. I realize you probably hear a lot of creative stories from people trying to scam their way into the club. And I'm certain it's no fun to have people approach you like they own the world and expect to be treated like it. But you don't look like the kind of gentleman whose mother raised him to disrespect women."

Lilah resisted the urge to giggle at the look of wide-eyed chagrin on his face. "I...uh...I—"

"Please tell me you're not giving my friends a hard time," a deep masculine voice called out behind them.

Lilah froze in place. She knew that voice. It couldn't be—

She turned and found herself looking up into a pair of deep-brown eyes. He towered over her at six-foot-four and was dressed in a black winter coat over an impeccably tailored, dark suit. His crisp, white shirt was open at the collar.

All of Lilah's words stuck in her throat.

"Mr. Martin, my apologies," the bouncer said, opening the rope for them to pass through.

Chapter 3

As he guided the two women past the entryway, Tyler Martin was pleased to have done his good deed for the day.

He hated velvet ropes, bouncers, celebrity parties and all the air kisses and fake smiles that went along with them. Helping these girls get past that thick-necked jerk redeemed some of the self-respect he'd lost profiting from this life.

But, on second glance, Tyler realized that he recognized these women. He'd be hard pressed to remember the name of the tall one with brightly colored hair, but he'd know Lilah Banks anywhere.

It was hard to forget the shy sixteen-year-old

who had sat at the kitchen table with him more times than he could count.

"I know you two, don't I?" He touched Lilah's arm. "You're Lilah Banks, right?"

Lilah started. "You know my name? You remember me?"

"Of course, you spent so much time at our house, our housekeeper thought you lived there."

Lilah laughed nervously and her friend stepped forward. "I'm Angie Snow, Lilah's best friend."

"Oh yes," Tyler said, shaking her hand. "I recognized your face."

He'd been two years ahead of the girls in school, so he was already in his first semester at the University of Maryland when Lilah started tutoring his brother.

His heart had gone out to her because it had been so obvious that she'd had a huge crush on Reggie. More often than not, she'd been stuck with him because his younger brother had his head in the clouds and rarely showed up for tutoring on time.

When Reggie had shown up, he wasted her time bitching about how hard things were around the house. Hard? The kid had everything handed to him on a silver platter. It was Tyler who picked up the slack. Shopping for food, running errands and driving the tutor home while Reggie played video games in his bedroom.

But, if Reggie was self-centered, he had no one

to blame but himself. Their mother was a doctor and their father a lawyer. So, although they always had every new gadget and video game, their parents were rarely home. Vivian Martin didn't like having strangers raise her kids, so when Tyler was old enough, Reggie became his responsibility.

Thank God he loved the kid. Which wasn't difficult since Reggie had a witty sense of humor and was genuinely fun to be around. He had an inherent charm that made it easy to forgive his mistakes. They were extremely close, which worked out well since their worlds were so tightly intertwined.

Reggie had a natural gift for music, and Tyler had a natural gift for business. While Reggie wrote songs in the recording studio, it was Tyler's job to handle the business details, including making sure the accountant, publicist and the rest of the industry didn't take advantage of his baby brother.

Which brought him to his present situation. He avoided the limelight whenever possible, but he'd come to accept that in this business, important meetings often took place in the VIP lounge of some popular night spot. He now represented several people in the entertainment industry, and tonight Reggie wanted him to meet a potential new client.

Now that he'd gotten them past the doorman, Tyler half expected the girls to float off. Instead they huddled close, with no obvious agenda.

The room—lit with pink, green and orange

neon lights showcasing wide decadent beds with drapes and pillows—was buzzing but not packed. He scanned the area for Reggie, but since he didn't see a crowd of fawning females, he knew Reggie wasn't in the room.

A DJ pumped mellow dance music through the speakers, loud enough to catch a rhythm but not so loud as to curb conversations.

"Um, you're probably wondering why you found us trying to crash this party, huh?" Angie started.

"Since you mentioned it…"

"We're kind of on a mission. Tell him, Lilah."

Lilah blanched and gave her friend a stunned look.

Tyler tried to break the ice. "Like a scavenger hunt?"

Lilah gulped. "Yeah, sort of. Um, when I was sixteen I made this list of things I wanted to do before I turned thirty."

Tyler nodded. He was thirty-two, which meant the big three-oh had to be just around the corner for Lilah.

"My birthday's in two weeks, and I thought it might be nice to finish off The List."

"And something on your list involves this club?" Tyler couldn't help noticing that Lilah seemed mortified. He wanted to ease her embarrassment, but he didn't know how when he didn't even know what she was trying not to say.

"A couple of things, actually." She pulled a PDA phone out of her purse and showed him the illuminated screen. "Crash a party and…uh, something else."

"What's the other thing?" He couldn't keep himself from asking.

"It's actually pretty convenient that we ran into you because it involves your brother Reggie," Angie said, trying to help Lilah along.

"Ah, I see…" He should have known.

If it were possible, Lilah seemed even more embarrassed. "Keep in mind, I started this list when I was sixteen." She scrolled her PDA screen and handed him the phone.

Item number one on her list was *date Reggie Martin*. For some reason that Tyler couldn't define, his heart sank.

He'd known she'd had a crush on his brother back in high school. He'd even tried to get his brother to acknowledge that fact, but he'd insisted that Tyler was reading too much into the situation.

Lilah rushed to explain herself. "I know it sounds absurd. He probably has a girlfriend or fiancée or something. I just thought, maybe, as a favor to a high school friend, we could have drinks or something. That way I can cross this off my list with minimal intrusion on his life."

Tyler couldn't help himself. He threw his head back and laughed. When he saw the hurt expression on her face, he immediately brought himself under control. "I'm sorry. Yes, he's single. I'm sure some sort of meeting that will qualify as a date won't be a problem."

Lilah was visibly relieved and Tyler felt his stomach muscles clench as she asked, "Is he here tonight? We heard that he might be here."

"Yeah, he's supposed to meet me here. He's probably in the VIP area, wherever that might be. Hold on."

Tyler pulled out his cell phone and punched the speed dial for his brother.

"Yo," Reggie answered with his standard greeting.

"Where are you? I'm at the club, and I don't see you."

"I'm downstairs in the VIP. Come down."

"Actually, I'm up here with a couple of women who would like to talk to you."

"Nice. Brother, you work fast. Are they hot?"

Tyler let his gaze slide over to the two women watching him expectantly. He turned his back, feeling heat creep up his neck. "Of course."

Angie, tall and willowy with her wild explosion of curls, was definitely beautiful, if you liked that funky art-student vibe. Lilah, on the other hand, was petite and curvy with luminous pale skin and honey-colored hair. She hadn't changed much since high school. In fact, if he hadn't known better, he would have sworn that she was still in high school.

The only really noticeable changes were her eyes. They no longer held the open invitation he used to see there. Now, they were clearly marked Do Not Disturb. She'd been burned by someone.

But then again, who hadn't? It was only a matter of time for most people anyway.

"Do you want me to bring them down?"

"Nah, if they're the clingy type, once they're in, I'll never shake them off. I'll come up. Give me ten."

"Great. We'll get a table…er, bed and wait for you."

He clicked the phone shut and turned back to the girls. "He'll meet us up here in ten minutes. I'll see about finding us a spot to hang out."

Angie shook her shoulder so hard, Lilah thought her arm might fall off. "See, this worked out just like I said it would."

Lilah snorted. "Not *just* like you said it would. Besides, it hasn't 'worked out' yet."

"Come on, what are the odds of Tyler Martin coming to our rescue of all people? For a split second, I actually thought it was Reggie coming up behind us."

"You're not the only one." Lilah decided that it was her state of shock that accounted for her sudden loss of breath at the sight of Tyler.

Her memory of him hadn't done him justice. She'd gotten the basic stats right in her mind's eye—tall, dark-skinned, the same chestnut-brown eyes that Reggie had. But the real beauty lay in the details.

He was so much taller than she'd remembered. Sure, she was all of five-foot-two herself, but Tyler seemed to loom in the night like a dark tower in a black overcoat. And his skin was dark, but it glowed like burnished wood—clear and smooth.

And those light-brown eyes were not so much brooding as she'd remembered, but intense. He'd always looked at her as though he could see everything inside her. Like she was emotionally naked before him. It was one of the things that she'd always found so disturbing about him.

She'd never thought of Tyler as handsome—certainly not compared to Reggie. But her memory had gotten that one wrong, too. He was definitely handsome. Not in the smooth-faced, curly lashed, flash-those-pearly-whites way that Reggie was good-looking.

Tyler simply had a face that was well put together. A strong jaw with just the hint of stubble, a nose that was pointed without being too sharp, deep-set eyes and thick lips, and his hair rounded into a tight, business-like fade.

Sexy. The word flashed in her brain and was gone, like a subliminal ad.

"We gotta get some drinks in you," Angie said,

tugging her arm. "You're so nervous you're practically catatonic."

"I'd rather have some food. I'm starving."

"This place is also a restaurant. I'm sure we can get you something, eventually. The drinks are necessary now. We have to make sure you can actually speak when Reggie gets up here. You're so stiff, you could be made of cardboard."

"We can't leave. Tyler's coming back for us."

"Fine. You wait here. I'll hit the bar. You still like appletinis, right?"

"Yeah, that's fine." Lilah's mind had already wandered off. In a matter of minutes, she was actually going to be talking to Reggie Martin.

She saw Tyler's tall, dark form emerge from the crowd. He came to her side, taking her elbow in his hand. Leaning down to her ear, he whispered, "I'm going to take you to bed."

Chapter 4

Lilah felt Tyler's breath on her ear as he spoke, and his words registered with a jolt. *I'm going to take you to bed.*

She jerked back from him, off balance from the unexpected erotic thrill tingling the base of her spine.

Tyler reached out and steadied her with both hands, preventing her from reeling back into a passing waitress with a tray full of drinks.

"I'm so sorry," Tyler said as she pulled herself together. "I should never have said that. I didn't mean to startle you. I was just trying to be clever. And it was an inappropriate remark."

"No, no. It was fine," she tried to reassure

him, feeling foolish for getting so flustered. "I can take a joke."

"Why don't we go sit down?" He looked around. "Where's your friend?"

"Angie went to the bar. Will she be able to find us if we get in be—uh, sit down?"

"I'll make sure she does," he assured her.

He began steering her toward one of the large beds along the far left of the room. A waitress helped them settle in by tucking their shoes in a drawer below and exchanging them for terry-cloth slippers emblazoned with the word Duvet.

Just as Lilah was awkwardly climbing onto the mattress, Angie arrived with two green apple martinis. Tyler helped Angie juggle the drinks as she took off her boots and joined them on the bed. Lilah and Tyler had checked their coats, but Angie insisted that hers was an integral piece of her ensemble.

Lilah quickly discovered that it was hard to recline comfortably and keep her cocktail dress from riding up. She finally arranged herself into a suitably modest position, wishing desperately that she'd worn pants.

"I'm not sure whose idea this was—" Angie started.

"I know. It's the worst," Lilah chimed in.

"—but, I love it," Angie finished at the same time.

"You don't like it? I think it's great." Angie was propped against the row of cream, satin pillows with her long legs stretched out in front of her. Her long jacket draped her legs.

Tyler looked right at home, too. He was stretched across the bottom of the mattress giving him plenty of room for his legs, as he propped his head on his palm. He would also have a bird's eye view of Lilah's underwear if she forgot herself and moved her legs.

"What brings you ladies to New York?"

"I live here," Angie answered. "I design costumes for a playhouse in Greenwich Village, and Lilah's just visiting for the next two weeks. We've got to check off the rest of her list before November 10th."

Tyler nodded. "That's a pretty ambitious task. How many things have you gotten done since you got to New York?"

Lilah chewed her lip. "I flew in this morning, first-class. That was one. And we crashed this party. That was two."

"So what's this big soiree for, anyway?" Angie asked, sipping her martini, then placing it back on the clear doughnut-shaped tray for drinks in the center of the bed.

"It's a corporate launch party for a new men's cologne called Isosceles." He pointed toward the center of the room, and Lilah noticed for the first time that there were large pyramid displays of tri-angular cologne bottles.

"Since Reggie's single is called 'Love Triangle' his publicist thought this would be a good opportunity for some cross promotion."

Lilah's heart sped up. "Will Reggie be performing tonight?"

"No. He agreed to make an appearance and sign copies of his single. He convinced a few of his boys to tag along, so I don't think he's planning to hang out here long."

"Damn, sounds like there aren't going to be a lot of other big celebrities here then?" Angie asked.

"No, I've seen a few Broadway actors and radio personalities, but for the most part this crowd is media types and corporate investors. It's safe to say that Reggie is probably the most famous person here."

Lilah felt her stomach growl and took a sip of her drink because it was the only thing on the table. "Aren't they supposed to have food here? Do you think we could get a menu?"

"The waitress told me that the restaurant is closed. They have some cold hors d'oeuvres and sushi, but I think that's it."

Lilah wrinkled her nose. She wasn't in the mood for anything cold. She wanted hot food in healthy portions. Forcing herself to relax, she took another sip of her drink. Reggie would be coming around shortly. After she pleaded her case to him, she and Angie could leave and get a real dinner.

"Are they giving out free samples of that cologne?" Angie wondered out loud. "Those little bottles are cute. I think I'm going to go over there and try to snag one."

Angie bounced off the bed and through the crowd, leaving Lilah and Tyler alone. Lilah tilted her glass and drained the last of her apple martini.

Her head swam a minute as the drink finally began to work on her empty stomach. Great, the last thing she needed was to be plastered by the time Reggie showed up.

But, on the upside, she was suddenly feeling one hundred percent less anxious than she had been just five minutes earlier. She leveled her gaze at Tyler, who had directed his attention to the plasma screen in the center of the room.

"Do you ever get back to the D.C. area?" she asked.

He turned to face her. "Not often. Our parents still live there, but since Reggie and I both live here, they prefer to come up."

"I guess that makes sense." Lilah tucked her feet under her body and leaned forward, smoothing her dress across her knees. "How did you both end up here? Did Reggie come first and you followed him?"

"No, after I graduated from Maryland, I came here to attend law school at Columbia. After trying his hand at a lot of day jobs, Reggie finally gave up and moved up here with me. Eventually he made some connections in the music business and the rest is history.

"I guess you could say I've been his business manager all his life, but in the last couple of years, as his career took off, managing his business started taking over my practice. I finally decided to manage him full-time, and recently I started taking on other clients."

"You both must be doing very well."

"What about you? You still live in D.C.?"

"Yeah, I just bought a condo in Georgetown."

"What do you do there?"

"I'm in the real estate business."

"That's great. How do you like it?"

"It's fine." Her answer came out like a half-hearted sigh.

Suddenly the fact that she was a very successful real estate agent didn't seem to count for much. Especially when she was surrounded by all these sparkling happy people.

Without thinking, Lilah reached for Angie's martini and gulped it down.

The fact remained that she was about to be thirty and her life was nowhere near where she'd expected it to be.

Time was bearing down on her like a freight train, and she was stalled on the tracks.

"Tyler?" The warm-colored lights straining

through the canopy's filmy curtains and the effects of the appletinis made her feel like she was in a cocoon. She felt secluded, despite the fact that there were clusters of people on the canopied beds all around them.

"Yes?"

"I'm going to be thirty in two weeks." Her voice shook with emotion.

He chuckled. "Okay, but you shouldn't worry about it. You don't look a day over eighteen."

She pursed her lips. "Why does everyone think it's a compliment to say that to me? I'm not a little girl. I'm a woman." Whew and she was *drunk!*

Lilah could hear herself and knew she sounded ridiculous, but she was powerless to stop.

"I can see that," he said huskily. "Trust me, no man in this room could miss that fact."

Lilah felt her face light up with embarrassment. His gaze had rested on the daring décolletage of her slinky dress. This conversation was definitely headed in the wrong direction.

In fact, it wasn't just the conversation. She was headed in the wrong direction. Seeing Tyler reclining on the end of the bed, taking her in with his hooded gaze, sent a hot pulse sizzling through her.

In her inebriated state, she was quick to remember just how long it had been since she'd been in proximity of a good-looking man and a bed. She had a sudden, wacky impulse to climb on top of him.

But two drinks hadn't made her bold enough for that. Her survival instincts were still intact. "Do you think Reggie will notice?"

Tyler straightened into a sitting position. "Of course, in fact, let me find out what's keeping him." He took his cell phone out of his jacket. "I need to find a better signal. Be right back."

Lilah didn't watch him walk away. The room was spinning. She lay back against the pillows and closed her eyes.

Tyler swore under his breath. Contrary to what many outsiders believed, tonight was the first time in history that Tyler had been jealous of his brother.

As a general rule, he and Reggie weren't even attracted to the same type of women. It's not that Reggie was particular. He wasn't. He liked them all shapes and sizes. On more than one occasion, his younger brother had tried to offer Tyler his leftover groupies. Tyler always refused.

Easy and available wouldn't do for him. He had a more discriminating eye. They had to be sophisticated, ambitious and intelligent. But he was a man. He liked them sexy with curves, too.

As a result of the brothers' differing needs, the two never fought over women—or anything else for that matter. Reggie wanted fame. Tyler just wanted success. Reggie wanted to make music. Tyler wanted to make money. They were like yin and yang. Perfect opposites, which made for a balanced relationship between them.

Until now.

For the first time Tyler felt himself coveting something that wasn't meant for him. Lilah Banks had walked into his life and captured his attention entirely. For the first time that he could remember, he'd been about to indulge in a serious public display of affection. And from the look on Lilah's face, he was certain she was on the same page.

Only the Martin man that she wanted was his brother.

So be it, Tyler told himself. He wasn't hard up for dates. He'd been casually seeing an attorney for the past few weeks. The best thing for him now was to find his brother and leave the rest to Lilah.

He no longer wanted to be involved. After finally finding a signal downstairs, outside the bathrooms, Tyler speed-dialed his brother.

"Yo."

"Where are you? You said you'd be up in ten minutes. You know what? It doesn't matter. I'm just going to bring the girls down to you, okay?"

"Uh, actually, bro, me and the boys are at the 40/40 club. I was just about to call you. Why don't you grab the girls and meet up with us here?"

"Are you kidding me? You left without telling

me? Why would you do that?" Tyler tensed. He was ready to launch into a lecture on wasting other people's time.

"The boys were getting bored. We had to roll quick so we wouldn't get caught by the fans. I didn't have time to come upstairs. The manager let us out the back door."

"You could have called me. The only reason I'm here tonight is to meet your friend. What happened with that?"

"He's here. Don't trip. Just come meet us."

"No, I'm done for tonight. Later." Tyler clicked the phone closed before his brother could respond. His anger would ebb quicker if he didn't have to hear the kid's voice right now.

Great. Now he had to go back to the girls and tell them they'd crashed this place for nothing. Oh well. He'd done what he could. Now he just wanted to get home and take a shower. Preferably cold.

As Tyler crossed the room, he saw that Angie seemed to be on the receiving end of an intense sales pitch from one of the Isosceles promoters. Climbing the steps to their bed, he froze, taking in Lilah's prone form.

Sleeping Beauty.

Her face was burrowed into one of the satin pillows and her feet were curled beneath her. Hair slipped out of her up-do to trickle down her neck.

For a fleeting second Tyler had the strong urge to curl up beside her and kiss her awake.

He shook it off. He wasn't Prince Charming in this fairy tale. That role was reserved for someone else.

Moving over to Lilah's side, Tyler gently lowered his weight onto the bed, careful not to startle her. He leaned over her and softly prodded her shoulder. "Lilah, wake up."

She murmured under her breath and rolled onto her back. Her eyes fluttered open and she gave him a sleepy smile.

"Lilah, I—"

She grabbed his lapel and jerked him downward. Tyler found himself sprawled across Lilah's body. Then she kissed him.

Wide-eyed, Tyler remained as still as stone as Lilah's lips explored his. Feeling his ardor resurface, he groaned in defeat and took over the kiss.

He didn't believe in public displays of affection, but no man in his right mind could resist this. She was soft and warm, and her lips had the faint tart taste of green apples.

His tongue surged into her mouth, and when he finally broke the kiss, she moaned in protest. "Reggie…"

Tyler's spine snapped straight and Lilah's eyes cleared. She was no longer lost in her sleepy alcohol-induced haze. Her eyes were filled with shock and confusion. She opened her mouth to speak….

Slipping his hand behind her neck, he kissed her with persuasive force. He felt Lilah's arms curl around him as she leaned into his embrace. Finally he pulled back to look into her eyes.

"My name is Tyler. And I don't want you to ever make that mistake again," he said just before his lips found hers.

Chapter 5

Lilah was having an out-of-body experience. There was no other explanation for the surreal dimensions her world had taken on.

Her fingers were caressing the ultrasoft skin on the nape of a man she barely knew. And she was loving it. Her mind began to cloud once again as the sensations of his lips working expertly on hers intensified.

Vaguely, in the distance, she knew she should be resisting. Something about the time and place was completely wrong. But logic couldn't penetrate the fog surrounding her.

"Whoa!"

Tyler released her and her head fell back against the pillows.

Lilah watched the scene unfold as though she were watching a movie. Tyler was sputtering while Angie gaped at them, her arms stacked with three boxes of Isosceles cologne.

"It's good to see the two of you getting to know each other better."

They both turned their attention to Lilah. "Are you okay, missy?" Angie asked.

Lilah felt the giggles bubble up from inside her. She pointed a finger at Tyler. "He—he is a good kisser!"

Angie dumped the boxes on the bed. "Okay, she's drunk. She's been telling me all night that she needed to eat something, and I should have listened to her. I'd better get her back to the hotel."

Tyler came to his feet. "I'll help you get a cab."

Moments later Lilah felt her shoes being shoved onto her feet. Tyler was standing back, watching her.

She gave him a big smile. "It was so nice sharing a bed with you."

There's someone in my bed! Lilah's mind screamed as she came into consciousness. As the world began to take shape around her, she realized she was lying in her hotel room and the body next to her belonged to Angie. There was no mistaking the soft, gurgling snore she'd endured all through college.

The clock radio on the night table read 1:22 a.m. Lilah sat up straight and a slow, steady throb began at her temple. She trudged to the bathroom for her toiletry case that housed her ibuprofen, and took a swig of water straight from the tap to swallow the pills.

"Oh, what a night," she whispered, sinking to the floor. A sting of heat rushed her cheeks as she remembered making out with Tyler Martin. "What the hell am I doing?"

She glanced out into her darkened hotel room and wondered, yet again, why she was even there. Lilah's mind began to fill with thoughts like a tub filling with water. A few moments more and she'd overflow. There was only one outlet for her when that happened.

Using the light from the bathroom, Lilah crept into the room and settled herself at the tiny desk where she'd set up her laptop. After connecting to the Internet, she pulled up her blog.

She'd first discovered online Web journals when she was updating the Web site for her real estate firm. She employed the technology then in hopes of generating repeat traffic to the site. Later, after her divorce, she'd begun a personal blog to cope with her sadness and frustration. To her surprise it had become a therapeutic outlet as other divorced women rallied around her blog until it ultimately evolved into a virtual support group.

She began her *Lilah's List* blog before coming to New York. She wanted to have a lasting memory of the experience. Now Lilah wasn't so sure she'd want to remember it. She was already off to a rocky start.

Feeling her embarrassment rising again, she began to type.

I made out with a stranger last night.

As she channeled the words through her fingers, Lilah was able to release her misgivings. Now it was as though it had happened to someone else, she thought as she completed her entry.

So, while my first day didn't go quite according to plan, it wasn't a total loss. I checked a whopping four items off The List!

30. Crash a party. Sure, Lady Luck tossed me a bone in the shape of Reggie Martin's brother, but at least I had the chance to give that bullying bouncer a piece of my mind.

28. Kiss a stranger. Which must be why I had so little of my mind left when I checked this one off. Tyler Martin wasn't a perfect stranger. But I hadn't seen him in over ten years, so I think it qualifies.

~~31. Do something scandalous.~~ I know it's not much by most standards, but I think making out with a virtual stranger in public is as scandalous as it gets for me.

~~43. Fly first class.~~ Blah. I may have to try this one again to see what it's like when you're not paralyzed with fear. But for now, check!

"What are you doing?"

Lilah had been so engrossed in her blogging that the sound of Angie's groggy voice nearly made her jump out of her skin.

"Nothing." Lilah hastily closed the laptop.

Angie leaped out of bed and rushed over. "Are you looking at porn?" She opened the screen and read it over her shoulder. "What's this? I didn't know you had a blog. I didn't even know you knew what one was. How come you never told me about this?"

"It's private."

Angie stared at her. "Yeah, you only share it with your gazillion closest friends on the World Wide Web."

"I mean, no one I know in real life knows about my blogs. It's just my way of sorting through my thoughts."

Angie turned away and sank down on the bed.

"What?" Lilah asked. "Why are you looking at me like that?"

"You're still *my* best friend," she said softly. "But I don't feel like I'm yours."

"What are you talking about? That's crazy. Of course you're my best friend."

"Then why are there so many things in your life you don't share with me anymore? I know we don't live in the same state anymore, but we're both on the east coast. New York is only an hour by plane or three hours by train. I can see if you don't want to invest in weekly long-distance calls, but if you're bothering to write down the details of your life in a blog, you could have let me know. I could have kept up-to-date with you that way."

Lilah was mortified. "I'm so sorry, Ang. I didn't mean to shut you out. I guess I'm one of those people that when things aren't going so well, I don't like to talk about it. I can share it with strangers because they don't really know me."

"Ever since the divorce I haven't known which way was up. And even before then, Chuck required my full attention. I felt like I had an obligation to make my marriage my priority. You see how that worked out. Now, when I look around, I feel like all I have is so much wasted time."

Lilah moved over to join her friend on the edge of the bed. "I'm sorry I haven't been a good friend to you over the last several years, Angie. I know it's not good enough. But it's all I've got."

Angie hugged her. "It's okay. I just want to remind you that you don't have to rely on a virtual world of strangers. I'm right here, and I always will be when you need me."

Lilah hugged her friend back, nearly choking on the emotions welling in her throat. The intense moment was instantly broken when her stomach released a loud groan of hunger.

Angie laughed. "We never did get a proper dinner. I know a burger joint with twenty-four-hour delivery."

"Really? I love New York."

Tyler stared unseeing at his computer screen. It was nearly noon on Saturday and he hadn't gotten much, if any, work done. Weekdays were for meetings and phone calls, but Saturday mornings, he liked to try to catch up on e-mails and light paperwork. Then he could have the rest of the weekend to himself.

But today he couldn't concentrate at all. His mind kept drifting back to Lilah. He felt like a jerk for taking advantage of a woman who had clearly been intoxicated. He should have pulled away from the kiss immediately, but she'd caught him off guard. But that didn't give him an excuse.

Tyler smacked his forehead as he did every time the embarrassment came flooding back to him. He could only imagine how she was feeling today.

There was only one way for him to make things up to her. He had to give her what she wanted. A date with Reggie.

If he knew his brother, and he did, Reggie would be in bed until something approaching three o'clock. Then, since he didn't have any other appearances scheduled for the weekend, he'd hang out in his apartment playing video games until he went out clubbing with his boys around midnight.

That would leave him plenty of room to have dinner with his old, high-school tutor. Tyler expected there would be some protesting, but now the kid owed him one.

Feeling much better now that he had something proactive to do besides mentally replay last night's embarrassment, Tyler typed the words Casablanca Hotel into his Internet browser.

Tyler had heard Angie name the hotel when he'd hailed a cab for them last night. After dialing the number, he asked to be connected to Lilah's room.

"Hello?" a sexy, sleep-roughened voiced purred into the phone.

"Lilah? I'm sorry, did I wake you?"

"T-Tyler?"

"Yes." His stomach muscles clenched at the way she breathed his name.

She cleared her throat, but she still sounded like a phone-sex operator. "No, we were up, but I admit, we haven't been up long."

We? Before he could ask the question out loud, she continued.

"Angie and I ended up ordering out in the middle of the night and didn't get back to bed until after 5:00 a.m."

"Oh, I didn't mean to disturb your rest, I was just calling to see if the two of you were free for dinner."

"Dinner? Um…"

"With Reggie," he added before the silence could stretch on, then tried not to be offended by her quick recovery.

"Actually, yes, we are free."

"Great. I'll try to get some reservations at Sapa for seven. Should we pick you two up at the hotel?"

"No, I'm not sure what our agenda is for the day, but we'll probably be out and about. It might be easier if we meet you there."

"Then it's a date."

There was an awkward moment of silence, until they both tried to fill it at once.

"Look, about last night—"

"I want to apologize for my behavior—"

They laughed.

"I'm sorry—"

"No, I'm sorry—"

They laughed again.

"It's clear that both of us weren't quite ourselves last night," Tyler finally said. "Why don't we just leave it at that?"

"That sounds like a good idea."

Tyler hung up the phone wondering why he actually felt worse than he had before he placed the call. But he didn't want to dwell on it. Lilah was only in town for a couple of weeks, and after he got her together with Reggie, he wouldn't have to see her again.

Maybe then he'd be able to stop thinking about her.

Reggie Martin hung up the phone, cursing his older brother under his breath. Why did he think he could order him around every minute of the day?

Tyler actually expected him to have dinner with some girl he supposedly knew in high school. His brother had mentioned her name but Reggie had already tuned him out, replaying the mind-your-own-business mantra he played whenever Tyler started telling him what to do.

Wasn't it enough for Tyler that he handled every other aspect of Reggie's life, including his finances—giving him an allowance like a twelve-year-old?

Reggie tossed the cordless phone onto the sofa and picked up his note pad, trying to get back to the lyrics he'd been writing. Even though he stared at the words on the page, his mind refused to pick up where he'd left off.

He was starting to feel like a caged tiger. Not just in the moment, but in his life. He'd finally reached a point where he could call himself successful. The first time his parents heard his single on the radio he thought he'd finally walked out of Tyler's shadow.

Sure, they expressed all the right sentiments, but along with those came all the usual comments.

The music business is plagued with drugs and debauchery, but thank goodness you have Tyler to keep you out of trouble.

What would you do without Tyler to help you invest those big paychecks?

You can't make a living singing your whole life, you need a long-term plan like Tyler.

His parents would never see him as anything other than his older brother's responsibility. And frankly, Reggie had no idea why Tyler continued to put up with it. How much fun could it really be to follow behind your little brother cleaning up his messes?

Reggie's friends assumed that Tyler must come down so hard on him because he was jealous of his popularity and musical talent. But Reggie knew better. He'd trade in both his easy charm and his singing voice for Tyler's brain. His brother was so smart he could do anything he wanted. There were probably a lot of things Tyler wanted to do other than managing Reggie's business affairs.

If Reggie knew what was good for both of them, he'd leave the city and head down to Atlanta. He could take up his buddy's offer to collaborate with Jermaine Dupri. Despite the positive buzz on his album, many of the critics were saying that his R&B ballads needed more of a hip-hop edge to compete with the reigning artists.

But Reggie knew his days of coasting were in the past. For the first time in his life he had a lot to lose. He was at the turning point where he could launch himself into superstardom or languish in the record bins as a one-hit wonder.

He couldn't afford to make a lot of risky moves right now.

No, the safest thing to do was to stay in New York where he had steady access to his brother's advice. After all, his parents were probably right, he could have ended up broke or strung out without Tyler constantly barking in his ear like a junkyard dog.

But that didn't mean he had to do every little thing his brother told him, Reggie thought.

Tonight's dinner, for instance. Reggie was sure he could come up with a good excuse to blow it off.

Chapter 6

As Lilah and Angie rode the elevator down to the lobby Saturday afternoon, Lilah was disappointed at how much of the day she'd allowed to get away. She'd planned to wake up early and go ice skating at Rockefeller Center before climbing to the top of the Statue of Liberty. But, with the clock swiftly approaching three o'clock, Lilah knew there wouldn't be time for both before meeting Reggie Martin for dinner.

As the elevator doors slid open, Angie poked her in the arm. "Take that sour look off your face. You're going to be in the city for two weeks. You don't have to cram everything in on one day."

"I know. I just don't like wasting time. If you didn't take such long showers—"

"Oh, don't start that again. I'm not the one who held us up. You're the one who couldn't leave until you created an ice skating playlist for your MP3 player."

The women laughed. Lilah stopped in front of the lobby doors. "So, what should we do first? Skating or the Statue of Liberty?"

"Come on, Lilah. We can knock out something like that next week. Let's do something more daring." She pulled a printout of Lilah's List from her pocket and studied it.

"Aha! Get a tattoo."

Lilah rolled her eyes. "I really don't *want* a tattoo. And I'm certainly not ready for that one right now. Besides, I'll need a couple of glasses of wine first. Or bottles…probably a whole barrel."

Angie laughed, but continued to scan The List.

"Why don't we go to the Statue of Liberty?" Lilah pressed.

"Okay, if not the tattoo then let's visit a fortune-teller. She can tell you how this whole trip is going to turn out for you."

"If I'm going to fail, do you think I really want to know today? My first full day in town?"

Angie looked exasperated. "You're just full of excuses, aren't you? You're going to have to do all of these things eventually, remember? That's why you're here. What are you waiting for?"

"Can I help you ladies with something?" a female voice called.

Both women turned to see they were standing only a foot away from the front desk. The clerk had probably overheard their entire conversation.

"Yes," Angie said.

"No thanks," Lilah said.

But to Lilah's horror, Angie was already smoothing the creased sheet out on the woman's desk. "Do you know where we can find a fortune-teller?"

"Angie!"

"Hush, it's either that or the tattoo shop."

The fair redhead, whose nameplate read Maureen, swiveled to tap on her keyboard. "Sounds like you ladies are planning to really live it up while you're in the city."

"Yes, but I'm native and she's visiting. This is her first real day here and we need an ice-breaker activity."

Maureen looked up from the computer screen. "If you want to show your friend New York with a twist, you should try the *Sex and the City* tour. Visit all the hot spots where Carrie and the girls hung out on the show."

"That sounds great, but the activity has to be from this list." Angie casually held out The List as though she wasn't baring Lilah's private life to a stranger. "We've got two weeks before her thirtieth birthday to get the rest of this stuff done."

Lilah was swinging back a pink Timberland to give Angie a warning kick when the clerk shrieked with delight.

"Oh, this is amazing. I've always wanted a life list. I just never took the time to write anything down." Maureen gripped Angie's wrist like an old girlfriend. "Does she actually know Reggie Martin?"

Lilah, who finally got tired of the two women talking about her as though she weren't there, elbowed Angie aside before she could answer. "Yes, I do. We went to high school together, and I'm supposed to have dinner with him tonight."

"That is a-maaa-zing!" Maureen shrieked again.

"You see. I think that's traumatic enough for one day. So I thought my friend and I could go to the Statue of Liberty or ice skate at Rockefeller Center today. You know, to calm my nerves."

Maureen reached over to grab a sheet of paper off her printer and handed it to Lilah. "No, you've got to see the fortune-teller. I don't know much about this kind of stuff, but we had a lady staying here about two months ago that swore up and down this woman is the real deal. It's a bit out of your way, but it could be worthwhile. Maybe she can point you in the right direction for your date with Reggie Martin."

Angie smacked the desktop. "Maureen, you are a lifesaver."

"Then you guys have got to come back here and tell me all about it. I'm off at six, but I'll be back at the front desk all day tomorrow. I've just got to hear about the psychic and especially your date."

Lilah felt heat rushing up her neck to flame her cheeks. "Well, if you're really interested…"

"Oh, I am," Maureen said. "A lot of people think you see it all working in the city, but to be honest with you, in a small hotel like this, most days are deadly dull."

"Then you might want to check out my blog where I document my adventures with The List."

Maureen eagerly took down the Web address and Lilah dragged Angie away from the desk before she could pull up the site.

As Angie looped her arm through Lilah's and directed her toward the cab stand, Lilah said, "FYI, The List is private. I don't want you flashing it around like it's some free-for-all invitation to a keg party."

"Uh, private? Once again, I'd like to remind you that you're writing all about it for billions on the Web."

"Once again, I'd like to remind *you* that I'll never have to face those billions of strangers."

"Look, you're doing a really cool thing here. Most people are going to want to help you, not judge you."

"I just don't want to have to keep repeating the story for everyone we meet."

"You need to change your attitude, Lilah. You're going about this grudgingly instead of embracing it. That's a setup for failure."

"That's not true—"

"Isn't the point of all this to find yourself? To have all these experiences before you get too bogged down in adult life to enjoy it? If you're going to approach each day like you did today, put yourself out of your misery and go back home."

Lilah felt as though she'd been smacked in the face and didn't say anything for several blocks as their cab flew through the streets of New York. Angie was a terminally upbeat person, so when Lilah received a lecture from her, it was a big deal.

The truth was she hadn't entered this adventure with her heart in the right place. But she *was* investing a significant amount of time and money into this trip, so she knew she should try harder to stay focused.

The problem was that she didn't know how to recapture the fearlessness of her youth. Now all she *had* were fears. Fear of making a fool of herself. Fear of failure.

Lilah had never imagined herself as someone who would one day be divorced. Yet, here she was.

Just look how horribly wrong things had gone when she was playing by the rules. She could only imagine how bad it could get without any.

As the taxi pulled up in front of a brownstone in a residential neighborhood, Angie and Lilah sat looking at each other.

Lilah leaned forward to the driver. "Sir, are you sure this is the right place?"

He pointed to the address on the building. "This is the location you gave me."

Lilah had been expecting something more obvious. Something that shouted fortune-teller with capital letters. At the very least a neon sign in the window. The two women got out of the cab and climbed the stairs.

Lilah hesitated before ringing the doorbell. She elbowed Angie. "Do you think the concierge could have made a mistake and sent us to the wrong address?"

Angie shrugged. "There's only one way to find out. Ring the bell."

Lilah was still worried she was in the wrong place when a twelve-year-old Indian girl answered the door. Lilah looked down at her printout. "Hi, is Sushma Ghira here?"

The girl stepped back from the doorway, turning to shout into the hallway, "Mom, you have customers!"

They followed the girl into the living room and took seats on the sofa. No incense burning or colorful scarves draping a table with a crystal ball. It was a typical urban flat, bathed in earth tones. Lilah could see another younger girl sitting at the kitchen table coloring. The utter normalcy dashed Lilah's cheesy fantasies.

A few minutes later a petite woman descended the stairs. She wore a red pullover sweater with khaki pants, and her feet were bare.

"Welcome to my home," she said with a heavy Indian accent.

Angie and Lilah rose to shake hands with the woman. Lilah took another look around and whispered, "We're sorry to barge in on you like this. I'm not even sure we're in the right place. The concierge at our hotel said—"

"Palm reading or tarot card reading? Is that what you're looking for?"

Lilah looked at Angie who just shrugged back at her. "Um, yes, I think so."

"Then you're in the right place. Come sit down." She led them through the kitchen and into another room, where a small table was set up in the corner. Sushma sat in a wing-backed chair against the wall and Lilah took the seat before the table in front of her. Angie took a seat on a chaise longue off to the side.

"What kind of answers are you looking for?"

"I don't know…I guess just…am I moving in the right direction with my life?"

"Okay. We'll do the tarot card. That will give you an overall view of your state of mind."

Lilah felt her palms growing clammy. Thank goodness they weren't going that route. "How does this work?"

The woman reached out and placed the deck in Lilah's hands. "Each card has its own meaning. You will shuffle these cards, thinking about your question. As you do this, your energies will direct the cards."

Lilah resisted the urge to roll her eyes as she shuffled. Even though the most rational part of her mind didn't believe in psychics, there was another part of her that desperately wanted it to work.

"Okay," she said, handing the cards back to Sushma. The woman then began spreading the cards on the table in a complex pattern.

Lilah gasped when Sushma pulled out a card depicting the grim reaper. "Oh no!"

"Do not worry. That card does not mean death in the literal sense. It's change. Laying the old to rest so that new can begin. You'll understand as I go through the reading."

Sushma began interpreting each card and its

place in the spread she laid out for Lilah. "This first card represents you, and it is The Empress. She indicates that you must follow your instincts, your intuition, to find your success."

Lilah watched with rapt attention as Sushma continued through the reading, drawing on each card to interpret the others. "And here are The Lovers. The most literal interpretation is a choice between two potential lovers. For you, it could be two men or just a choice between two paths. The choice is yours, but you'll only grow if you choose wisely."

A choice between two potential lovers? Lilah had an instant flash of Tyler's warm lips. A choice between two brothers?

Somehow she knew that wasn't quite what the woman had said, but her mind locked in on the idea, even as Lilah tried to push it away.

When Sushma finally finished the reading, Lilah's head was spinning. She couldn't remember all the nuances of what she'd just been told.

The other woman must have sensed her confusion, because she said, "This is what you need to remember from all of that. You'll come to a crossroads and a choice must be made. It could be a choice between two men or just two ways of living. Either way, there will be conflict and change. Even the right choice won't be easy, so you must stay committed. Let your heart guide you through the fear. New growth and new opportunity await, if you choose wisely."

Lilah nodded and thanked the woman, unsure of what to make of what she'd just been told.

"What a crock," Angie said later when they were back in the taxi.

Surprised, Lilah looked up at her. "Really?"

"You ask her if your life is going in the right direction, and she tells you all this BS about crossroads and choices. They just rearrange and regurgitate the same drivel to everyone…new growth and new opportunity. Whatever. I guess she suckers people in with that accent. Oh well, I guess it was kind of fun, anyway, right?"

"Yeah." Lilah felt her cheeks stinging with embarrassment because she'd completely bought the woman's speech. It might not have made sense to Angie, but the reading really resonated with Lilah.

In fact, it tied in with what her best friend had told her on the way over. She could either dive into this opportunity with both feet or play it safe and head back home. But, she certainly couldn't keep on wandering along halfheartedly.

She had a chance most people weren't afforded. Two weeks to grab all the life experiences she could. In the recent past when she'd been presented with a choice to either play it safe or take a chance, she'd chosen safe.

Well, her first choice had just been made. Lilah was going to take a risk.

Chapter 7

I'm not sure if it's wise to indulge the whims of your youth at the ripe old age of twenty-nine. You see, this is how I ended up with an unusual tattoo in an unusual place.

As Tyler stepped through the entrance to Sapa restaurant, he realized he was early. He'd planned to hang back, perhaps arrive fashionably late, but he was actually eager to get the evening under way.

He'd chosen the restaurant knowing that Lilah

would appreciate the dramatic lighting combination of hanging lanterns and candles. It could be very romantic.

Tyler blew out his breath, reminding himself that they weren't here for that. Was this a classic case of wanting something he couldn't have? Because this borderline obsession he was developing for Lilah was uncharacteristic.

He walked over to the bar, hoping a stiff drink would put him in the right frame of mind. Before he could place an order, his cell phone rang. His brother's number flashed on the screen.

"Reggie?" he answered.

"Yeah, I've got some bad news, bro."

Tyler gritted his teeth. "Just don't tell me you're not coming."

"I can't make it. This is the only night I can meet up with Max in the studio."

"Reggie—"

"I know what you're going to say, but aren't you the one always preaching that my music has to come first? Well, that's what I'm doing. I need to lay down a dance track if I want the DJs to spin 'Love Triangle' in the clubs."

Unfortunately, Tyler couldn't argue with that. Which made him want to all the more. "Why can't you just—"

"I'm going to have to catch you later, man. Studio time isn't free."

Tyler clicked his phone closed, unsure what to do with the frustrated energy coiling inside him. For the second time now, Reggie had put him in a position of not being able to deliver on his word.

Why did Lilah want to date a guy like that anyway? If they got together for real, it would just be more of the same. On the other hand, *he* would never—

Whoa. His thoughts were headed down the wrong track again. Lilah wanted a date with Reggie. He was the one she'd had a crush on in high school....

Never mind that Reggie would never be able to appreciate a woman like her. Not the way Tyler could.

That sentiment was reinforced as he watched Lilah walk through the door before Angie. Under her brown leather jacket, she wore a velvety-black V-neck sweater that begged to be touched, and a pair of hip-hugging black jeans and low-heeled black suede boots. Her hair flowed in curls from a high ponytail and her cheeks were rosy from the October chill.

She looked cute. And sweet. And in that moment, Tyler felt a longing like he'd never felt before. What was it that was pulling him to her despite his better judgment? There was definitely something between them, and it was more than their impromptu make-out session the night before.

He'd felt it when she was in high school. It hadn't been romantic then. But it had been nice to talk to someone who didn't want something from him. Even though he was in college, she'd been able to grasp the complex social issues he'd wrestled with at the time.

Tyler had been going through a brooding phase where all the political injustices of the world weighed heavily on his young mind. It had been part of his nature, at the time, to debate everything, but she'd held her own in their discussions.

Now, years later, he couldn't remember anyone that had been as easy to connect with.

Lilah spotted him right away, walking over and catching him in a one-armed hug. "There you are. This place is gorgeous."

Angie came up on his other side and did the same. Tyler was sandwiched between two beautiful women, and he no longer minded that Reggie wasn't coming.

But he had to get the dirty work out of the way. "I have bad news, ladies. Reggie's not going to be able to make it tonight. He couldn't get away from the studio after all."

Tyler waited to hear a sigh of disappointment, but Lilah just shrugged it off, looking strangely relieved. "Oh well, I guess it's just the three of us then. Do you think you can handle two women on your own?"

Before Tyler could respond, the hostess motioned

for them to follow her to their table. Tyler trailed behind the women feeling his sense of anticipation rising.

Lilah was giving off a confident vibe that was a far cry from the guarded woman he'd met last night. Although she'd loosened up considerably after a couple of appletinis, she'd remained a bit melancholy. Tonight she was all smiles and sass as she slid into their booth.

Tyler situated himself across from the two women and picked up his menu to force his eyes away from Lilah. It was important not to rush things after last night.

"I have to tell you, Lilah," Angie said, studying her friend. "That psychic must have worked some kind of mojo on you after all because you've been a bundle of energy ever since."

"Psychic?" Tyler asked.

"Yup," Lilah answered. "Number 21 on The List—visit a fortune-teller."

"How did it go? Did she tell you anything useful?"

"It sounded like a bunch of mumbo-jumbo to me," Angie said.

"She didn't put a spell on me or anything. I actually decided to take *your* advice, Angie. I have an amazing opportunity to do some things I've always wanted to do. I have to stop worrying about the consequences, and just go for it."

Tyler smiled at Lilah. So he hadn't been imagining it. She really was shining from the inside out. "So, besides the psychic, what else did you girls do today?"

"From The List, just the psychic," Lilah said.

"Yeah, but afterward Lilah treated us both to manicures and pedicures." Both women held out their hands to be admired.

"Very nice," Tyler said dutifully.

"Meeting with your brother was supposed to be the other item I checked off today. That would have been a big one, so I guess I need to pick out another big thing to do instead."

Angie pulled out The List and spread it out in the middle of the table. "How about going to a karaoke bar? I think there's one on the lower west side."

Lilah stared at The List, shaking her head. "No, I need something bigger. I think I've got to bite the bullet on the tattoo."

Angie squealed with delight.

"Wow." Tyler raised his brows. For some reason he hadn't been expecting that. "So what's it going to be? The classic lower back tattoo you girls seem to love? Or maybe a sexy ankle tattoo?"

She sighed. "I don't know yet. I think I may need a few appletinis first."

"Oh no, my dear," Angie said. "You are cut off. After last night, nothing stronger than diet soda for you."

"Look who thinks she's my mother now." Lilah rolled her eyes and leaned toward Tyler. "I don't actually want a tattoo anymore, but it's on The List, so I'm committed to doing it. All I know is, I'd better get it over with before I chicken out."

Tyler imagined Lilah stretched out at the tattoo shop, her jeans pulled low, exposing that golden skin at the base of her spine. "This sounds like a very important, not to mention permanent, decision. I think I'd better come along as a consultant."

"Really? You want to watch?" she asked.

"You bet."

"Okay, I could use the extra moral support."

"Let me see this list." Tyler reached for the sheet of paper that was still sitting on the table in front of Angie. "Maybe there are other things I can help with."

As Tyler scanned through The List, he couldn't resist glancing up at Lilah. He saw a blush tinge her cheeks as she realized what he was probably reading.

A new resolve solidified in his mind. Lilah would be his.

He'd spent a lifetime putting his brother first. Why couldn't he have just this one thing for himself? If Lilah proved resistant to his seduction, he'd bow out. But he owed it to himself to see if there could be something real between them.

Reggie had already passed up his chance with her, and it wasn't as though he'd been pursuing her. So why would he care?

Besides, it seemed Lilah would be in need of a man to complete her list, and Tyler was more than willing to apply for the job.

Tyler and Angie helped Lilah out of the cab as she gingerly tried to stand alone. "That was the most traumatizing experience of my life."

Lilah knew she was being a tad melodramatic but, to her surprise, she was still feeling quite a bit of pain.

"Stop whining, you crybaby. It wasn't that bad," Angie said, pulling her through the diner door Tyler held for them.

Lilah gasped. "Says the woman who has no tattoos of her own. That may very well be the worst pain of my life. Well…besides a tooth-ache…and menstrual cramps and—"

"Then maybe you shouldn't have gotten it in such a sensitive area. I still think a shoulder would have been more practical."

"And have people see it every time I wear a sleeveless blouse? I don't think so."

"People are still going to see it whenever you lie on the beach. And since you love to tan that fair skin of yours, if you lie on your back, it's in full view for all the world to see."

Lilah was grateful that Tyler was politely ignoring the ludicrous banter that had been going on between them since they left the tattoo shop. While they had continued their debate in the cab, he had given the driver directions to an all-night diner. This, so Lilah could order the pancakes she'd been promised for being a good girl and holding still for the nice tattooist.

The out-of-the-way diner wasn't jam-packed at nearly midnight. There was a line, but it was moving quickly.

"The important thing—" Lilah announced "—is that now I can cross getting a tattoo off my list. I can tell my grandchildren it was a byproduct of my reckless youth."

Angie snorted. "Oh yeah, they'll really think reckless when they see that thing."

"Okay, maybe not reckless. But you were the one who said it needed to be meaningful. Something that would help me remember this adventure."

"And that tattoo reminds you of this adventure how?"

"It symbolizes happiness—exuberance, effervescence, ebullience even."

"Well, if it's such a symbol of joy for you, then you should have gotten it someplace where *you* could actually see it."

"I can see it."

"Not without a mirror or some interesting contortions."

Lilah looked to Tyler for help, but he still wasn't paying them any mind. Now, he was quietly asking the hostess for a table for three.

As Lilah slid into the booth beside Angie, she groaned. "It feels so good to get off my feet."

Angie released an exasperated sigh, and as Lilah met Tyler's gaze, he gave her a look of barely contained laughter.

"I must say, this has been quite an experience. I'm so glad you ladies let me tag along."

"No problem, I needed the extra help holding her down."

Lilah poked her friend in the arm. "Once again, I didn't see you lining up to join me in that chair. I think Betty Boop would have been cute on your ankle."

"Nope, this is your adventure, not mine," she answered without lifting her head from the menu. "But if I ever did get a tattoo, I'd get something much more exciting than—"

"All right, ladies, that's enough. Do you two always bicker like this?" Tyler asked.

Lilah exchanged a look with Angie, and then they answered him in unison. "We're not bickering."

Tyler stared at the two of them for a moment then picked up his menu in surrender. "My mistake."

Lilah and Angie laughed.

Lilah didn't know what to make of Tyler's easy acceptance of her banter with Angie. Chuck would have been chiding them to be quiet long ago. He hated when they yammered on, claiming their chatter gave him headaches. Tyler didn't seem the least bit annoyed. Instead he seemed…genuinely pleased to be in their company.

"But seriously," Angie said. "The smiley face is cute."

"Thank you," Lilah said, lifting her chin. "And I still think the bottom of my heel is an ideal place for it. No chance of *that* skin sagging with age."

"Sagging with age—that sounds like my cue," the gray-haired waitress said in her heavy Jamaican accent. "Welcome to Diamond Diner. My name is Belle, and I'll be your server tonight. Can I take your orders?"

They each rattled off their selections as Belle stood listening. After Lilah ordered her much-anticipated short stack of buttermilk pancakes, she couldn't resist asking, "Belle, aren't you going to write that down?"

"No, child. My skin might be saggin' with age and my hair gray to the roots, but I've got a mind like a steel trap. It may be rusty, but it still works."

She then went on to recite all their orders word for word—prompting the three of them to applaud when she finished.

"Don't be too impressed, children. My tired old brain just replaced the memory of my wedding night with 'coffee, two creams and no sugar.'"

The three of them roared with laughter.

After Lilah polished off her pancakes down to the last pearl of maple syrup, she held her stomach. "I'm so full, I may never eat again."

Belle chuckled as she leaned over to clear her plate. "Don't fret, honey, as far as I can tell, never comes around every four to five hours, so I'll be seeing you again."

Lilah smiled at Tyler. "I love this place. How come it's not overrun with people?"

He shrugged. "It's more of a hangout for the locals. It hasn't caught the eye of most tourists yet. So, you better keep the secret or Angie and I will have to revoke your trial membership."

"Membership to what?"

"The New Yorker's club. It provides access to all the places we locals don't want you tourists to know about."

"Oh, well aren't I lucky," Lilah joked.

"So what's on the agenda for tomorrow?" Tyler asked.

Angie shrugged and pointed at Lilah, who pulled out her PDA to check The List. "Tattoo—check. Fortune-teller—check. Ooh, I see a good one that I can check off right now. Number 33."

Angie read over her shoulder. "'Leave a $100 tip.' Great idea. Belle is the best."

Tyler smiled. "I think that would really make her day."

After they paid the check with the cashier, Lilah walked back to the table, leaving five twenty-dollar bills. Still reluctant to put her full weight on her tattooed foot, she followed Angie and Tyler out of the diner at a hobble.

As Tyler headed out to the street to hail a cab, Lilah noticed a gigantic man smoking a cigarette by the door. She recognized him immediately.

"Do diners have bouncers now, too?"

Chapter 8

"No, I'm just waiting for my mother to finish her shift." The bouncer from Duvet lowered his cigarette and stared at Lilah as if he knew her but couldn't place her.

Angie, who'd been behind Tyler as he walked into the street to hail a taxi, had turned around and was heading back to Lilah's side.

"That one," he said pointing at Angie: "I remember her."

Angie placed a hand on her hip. "As well you should. You called me chopped liver," she said, becoming indignant all over again.

The bouncer looked her up and down, from her

black motorcycle jacket and belted red knee-length sweater to her black leggings and red ankle boots. "I must have been crazy," he said with obvious appreciation.

Angie bristled under the bouncer's sudden change of heart. Lilah looked over her shoulder to see that Tyler had hailed a cab. Realizing the girls weren't behind him, he walked back toward them.

Just as he reached Lilah's side, the diner door flew open and Belle burst out onto the pavement.

"There you are!" she shouted, grabbing Lilah by the shoulder.

The bouncer rushed forward. "Mama, what's wrong? What happened?" He turned a menacing eye on Lilah. "What did you do to my mother?"

"Nothing! I—I—" Lilah's heart hammered in her chest.

Tyler stepped forward to get in between Lilah and the bouncer, and slipped a protective arm around her shoulder, but Belle was already pushing her son back, "Hush, Remy."

Belle thrust a fistful of cash into Lilah's hands. "You left your money on the table."

Lilah pushed the money back at her. "No, that's your tip."

Belle's brow was lined with confusion. "There must be some mistake. Your bill was only twenty-four dollars." She held up the money. "You left over four times that."

Lilah shook her head. "No, this is for you. I've always told myself that one day, when I received really great service, I would leave an outrageously good tip. That day finally came for me, Belle. I wanted you to have this for working so hard and making us laugh."

For a moment the older woman stood speechless, staring at the money in her hands. "How can I thank you?"

Remy stepped forward. "You gave my mother a hundred-dollar tip?" He shook his head, tapping his fist over his heart "One love. You're good people. You'll always be VIP with me. Come to the club any night you want, and I'll get you in free."

Lilah felt Tyler lower his arm from around her shoulders. She missed it right away, but knew it wasn't the right time or place for thoughts like that.

"Thanks, Remy, but that's not necessary," Lilah said. "I understand it's your job to keep riffraff like us out of your respectable establishment. But I'm sure Angie wouldn't mind an apology for calling her chopped liver."

Remy opened his mouth but Belle was already on him. "Remington Alfonso King—what is this I hear? You were rude to a woman? Calling her names?"

"Mama, you know I sometimes have to get tough at work. It's part of the job."

"You apologize right now."

Remy hung his head. "Yes, Mama."

Lilah giggled under her breath, watching the sheepish giant all but kneel at Angie's feet.

When he'd apologized to his mother's satisfaction, she excused herself to get back to work. But not before taking the time to thank them each profusely and to welcome them to eat in her section anytime.

With his mother gone, Remy turned his attention back to Angie. "A woman as fine as you are could never be chopped liver. You should let me make it up to you. Personally."

Angie waved him off. "Okay, that's enough of that, big boy. You're not my type."

"I can be any type you want...."

Lilah tuned out the rest of their banter as Tyler turned to face her. "What happened? I was getting a cab and then I saw you two getting into it with this guy again."

Lilah laughed. "It was funny because I came out of the diner and saw him standing by the door, so I asked him if diners have bouncers now, too. He told me he was just picking his mother up after her shift. He was staring at us like he didn't know who we were, so I reminded him. That's pretty much all that happened before you showed up and Belle came rushing out."

"I see. You had me worried there for a minute.

You're not one of those girls who attracts trouble everywhere she goes, are you?"

Lilah paused to consider that for a moment. She nodded. "You know, I think I just might be. You'd better watch out."

Before Tyler could respond, their attention was pulled away by Angie's squeal.

"You have a motorcycle? That's perfect. We need a motorcycle."

Sunday afternoon Lilah made Angie take her to a craft store where she bought all the supplies she would need to teach herself to knit.

They walked into the hotel lobby and Maureen, the front desk clerk, immediately waved them over. "I've been waiting all day to find out. How did your date go with Reggie Martin?"

Lilah set down her shopping bag and leaned against the counter, shaking her head. "He had to bail out at the last minute."

"Aw," Maureen said, looking positively crushed. "That's awful. Did he say why?"

"I didn't speak to him, but we had dinner with his brother who's also his business manager. He said he couldn't get away from the studio."

"What a bummer."

"She did get a tattoo, though," Angie chimed in.

Maureen perked up right away. "Oh my gosh. That's so cool. What did you get? Can I see it?"

Lilah bent down and untied her pink boots, pulling off her sock. "Not what you were expecting, was it?" Lilah said, flipping up her heel.

Maureen was stretched over the counter examining her foot. "How cute. Why did you get it there?"

Lilah shuffled her weight, struggling to put her boots and socks back on, while Angie answered. "She didn't want to get the tattoo anywhere that it might come back to haunt her in later years."

As Lilah rose, she saw Maureen marking on a sheet of paper. "What have you got there?"

Maureen held up Lilah's list. "I printed it out from your blog. You know, it's really entertaining. You're a good writer. Is that what you do for a living?"

"No, I'm in real estate."

"Oh. Well, anyway, I wanted to follow along with you as you check things off."

Lilah felt her embarrassment rising. "Seriously?"

"Yeah, did you get anything else done yesterday?"

Angie pulled out her own copy to compare with Maureen's. "You're missing Numbers 29 and 33. She's working on *learn to knit* today, but she's probably not going to get very far, so I'll get back to you on that one."

Lilah stared incredulously at the two of them poring over her private life as though it were a board game. Finally she just rolled her eyes and headed for the elevator.

Lilah didn't know what she was getting so worked up about. Two people reading her blog was no big deal. It wasn't like she had all the eyes of New York City on her.

Besides, with so much to do and so little time, she'd need all the help she could get.

Later that evening, Lilah was sitting cross-legged on the bed, while Angie had made herself at home at the desk. "Are you sure you want to devote the entire day to trying to knit?" she asked, pulling out a pad of paper.

Lilah was spreading her knitting needles, yarn and instructions over the bed. "I've never knitted a thing in my life. It could take a while for me to grasp the concept."

"Fine, while you work on that, you have to tell me what you want for your party."

"What party?" Lilah asked, frowning at the weapon-like knitting needles.

"Duh, your birthday party. And before you say you don't want one, refer to The List. Number 26, 'throw a wild party.'"

Lilah looked up and rolled her eyes. "How wild can a party of two really get? I don't know anyone here in the city."

"First of all, you know good and well a party

of two can get pretty wild. Remember your pre-bachelorette party?"

"Riding around Annapolis in a limo, with our heads sticking out the sunroof, trying to recruit future naval officers for the evening does not constitute a party."

"It most certainly does. We got a lot of takers."

"Sure, but we drove two blocks, came to our senses and kicked them out."

"That's only because we knew the rest of the girls wouldn't fit in the limo with all those sailors. If we'd wanted to, we could have had a pretty wild time just you, me and those naval cadets."

Lilah sighed. "So what exactly are you suggesting? That we spend my birthday driving around New York in a limo, picking up strange men?"

"Now there's an idea," Angie said, to which Lilah rolled her eyes.

"Never mind, you don't need to pick up strange men. You know Tyler Martin, and you're soon to get reacquainted with Reggie. The promise of him alone could pack a house."

"Okay, let me repeat this. I don't want to have a party with random people off the street."

Angie tapped her pen on her forehead for a second. "You let me worry about the guest list. The first order of business is always location."

Lilah shrugged. "This room is way too small

for any kind of party, and I've seen your apartment. It's even smaller than this hotel room."

"We could rent some place."

Lilah shook her head. "No, I don't want to spend that kind of money. Maybe it can be just a cocktail type of thing. We could meet in a bar and have a few drinks. Like Happy Hour."

"You're thinking too small. Wild party, remember? The active word there is wild. In fact, this hotel is cute, and I appreciate its charms, but you need something much more decadent for your birthday celebration."

"Angie—"

"I think we should get you a penthouse suite in a ritzy hotel for the night of your birthday."

"Do you think I'm made of money?"

Angie snorted. "Actually, yes. I think you've got to stop living like you're poor. You make crazy money in real estate, and I happen to know you're just sitting on that money from the sale of your house. It's nice to be frugal, but come on, girl. Live a little."

Over the years Lilah had gotten in the habit of downplaying the money she made because it had made Chuck uncomfortable. He'd hated that he hadn't made nearly as much selling insurance as she had in real estate. To placate his ego, they'd lived off his wages and had put hers away for a rainy day.

Lilah stared at Angie. "But what if—"

"I'm not asking you to break the bank, just loosen your purse strings a bit. I'm willing to do my part, but if you're in for a penny, you're in for a pound. You're going to be thirty. You've got to bring it in with a bang, right?"

Lilah felt a little sizzle in her blood. It could be really fun to have an elegant affair to commemorate her milestone birthday.

But what was the use of going to all that trouble if there weren't going to be any guests?

"Maybe we could invite some of my friends from D.C.? It's only a four-hour drive and a little less by train."

"Now you're talking. Just let me know who you want, and I'll take care of the rest."

Lilah sat up straighter, starting to get excited. "And if it's going to be in a penthouse suite, we should definitely have it catered."

"Yeah," Angie said, scribbling on her pad.

"And I've always wanted to have an ice sculpture. Maybe a giant number thirty. No, how about a male torso…even better just the—"

"Save that for your next bachelorette party."

Yeah, not much chance of her having another one of those. "Now, let's talk music. Do you think that suite will be large enough to fit a live band?"

Angie rolled her eyes. "I've created a monster."

Chapter 9

Monday evening Lilah stumbled into her hotel lobby, drained and soaking wet. She was tempted to collapse to her knees and kiss the marble tiles at her feet.

Maureen, who was working the front desk, called out to her. "Lilah, are you okay?"

She dragged herself over to the desk, using it as support as she slipped her feet out of her sopping shoes. "Why is it so difficult to get around this city?"

"What do you mean?"

"I took a cab downtown because I wanted to see Ground Zero. But, I think all the New York cabbies are out to get me."

"That's not true," Maureen said, winking at her. "They're out to get everybody."

"I'm not kidding. The first cab I got into at the airport was reckless and drove crazy-fast. Then the taxi Angie and I took back from the fortune-teller's on Saturday dropped us off two blocks from the hotel because he wanted to pick up a bigger fare that came in over the radio. And this guy today tried to rip me off, driving in circles to jack up the price."

"Aw, Lilah, why didn't you take the subway? There are stops all over the city, and it's much cheaper."

"That was my next bright idea. I thought there's no way I'm going to risk my life standing on the street corner trying to hail a taxi back uptown, so I tried the subway."

Maureen got a wary look on her face. "What happened?"

Lilah shook her head at the memory. "I didn't know I was mentally challenged."

"What?"

"I swear to you, until today I thought I was at least as smart as the average person. But I just couldn't figure out the subway. The first stop I went to didn't have a train running to Times Square. The nice lady in the little booth tried to direct me to another subway stop—not far away, she said—where I could pick up the right train."

Maureen was now resting her face in her hands and wincing. "And?"

"And I never found it. I walked for blocks, and I couldn't find this phantom subway station the woman had directed me to. When I finally found another one, I realized that I had wandered much farther away from my destination. So, fine, I bought my ticket and I found the right-lettered train, but it was going the opposite direction. Great, I figured all I have to do is get to the other side. I took the only exit I could see and found myself standing back out on the street. Fare wasted without riding anywhere."

"Oh, Lilah—"

"At this point, I was so frustrated that I figured I'd just take my chances with another cab. Of course, by now it's raining and none of them would stop for me. When I finally found a cab to pick me up, he went around the block and picked up two more passengers. I rode all the way uptown crammed beside two sweaty men."

"I'm not sure that's even legal," Maureen said, shaking her head. "You've had some rotten luck, haven't you?"

She reached into her drawer and pulled out a business card. "Here."

Lilah read the name. Sanjay Mumbari. "Who is this?"

"He's a young man who was in here early in the

week trying to drum up some business for his car service. I don't normally support gypsy cabs, but this guy seemed really sincere. He's just starting out, so you could probably get him to drive you anywhere you'd like without too much advance notice."

"Uh, thanks," Lilah said, shoving the card into her handbag. "Right now, all I want is a hot shower. See you later," she said as she walked to the elevator.

It had been a trying day, but it wouldn't have been nearly so bad if she could have gone through it with someone else.

That was the hardest thing to adjust to since the divorce—doing everything alone. Angie'd had to work and Lilah hadn't wanted to waste the day in her hotel room by herself.

Walking the streets hadn't been a big deal during the day, despite watching the tourists comprised of couples and families exploring the city. But once it had gotten dark, Lilah had begun to realize just how vulnerable she was.

She knew that Angie's life didn't stop just because she was in town, and that, if she wanted to get through The List, there were things she was going to have to do on her own.

But as Lilah let herself into her room and stretched out on the bed, it was hard not to feel lonely. It would have been nice to have someone else to curl up next to her.

* * *

By the next morning Lilah had pushed her melancholy aside. It was a new day.

Yesterday felt like a wash, because she had nothing new to add to her blog. No one wanted to read about her disasters in knitting. Today, she needed to make something happen.

Spending so much time with Angie lately reminded Lilah how much she had changed over the years. She'd been proactive. A doer. Lately she'd been sitting back and letting life happen to her. She needed to take control.

Tyler had tried to get Reggie to the restaurant to meet them on Saturday, but that had fallen through. The old Lilah wouldn't be sitting around waiting for another door to open.

The old Lilah would punch her way through a wall.

Sitting down at her computer, Lilah ran a Google search for Reggie Martin's name. After wading through fan pages and celebrity gossip, she finally came across a useful bit of information.

She had the name of his publicist, Manny Lupinsky.

Angie was always telling her that she could talk her way through anything. Lilah hadn't earned the top sales honor at her real estate firm by accident.

So without hesitating she picked up the phone. After a brief conversation with his receptionist, she was being transferred to Reggie's publicist's voice mail.

"Hello, Mr. Lupinsky. This is Lilah B-brown with Hot—" she paused "—Pocket Jeans. We're very interested in using your client Reggie Martin in a full-page ad campaign for our jeans. We'd love it if you could arrange a meeting with us and your client to discuss it." Lilah left her cell phone number and hung up.

What had she just done? Lilah shook off her reservations. She couldn't wait to tell Angie—she would be so proud of her.

Tuesday evening, Reggie Martin looked through the glass studio window at his brother. He'd had to twist his arm to get Tyler to come there. For some reason, Tyler was still ticked off because he'd missed dinner Saturday.

What was the big deal? Something about meeting some girl he used to know? His brother didn't usually care how he dealt with fans.

Reggie shrugged it off. Tonight probably wasn't the best possible time to talk to Tyler about Atlanta. But the more he thought about it, the more he felt like he needed a change.

Tyler always wanted him to take things slow, but Reggie never would have gotten his break if he hadn't taken a big risk. His gut was telling him to go for it.

On the other hand, without Tyler's support he would have drowned out here in the city. Maybe he already had everything he needed. After all, it was New York City. How could Atlanta compare to that?

He and his producer, Max, had put in a lot of work over the last few days to pull together a funkier hip-hop track for the dance clubs. It wasn't quite the sound he was hoping for, but maybe this would be good enough. He needed Tyler's opinion.

When it came to his music, no one was a bigger supporter than Tyler. If *he* thought the track was hot, then maybe Reggie would have a chance.

"All right, Max, hit it."

Music filled his headphones and Reggie closed his eyes and let the words flow through him.

Tyler's neck snapped up when Reggie started singing. The smooth melodic quality of his voice brought him back to the first time he saw his brother on stage. He wasn't ashamed to admit it had brought tears to his eyes.

This was what it was all about. This is exactly what Tyler admired about Lilah and her list— taking your dreams and making them reality. That was one of his goals when he began to study law. He'd wanted to make things happen for people who couldn't get there on their own.

The entertainment business may not have been his vision when he started law school, but moments like this made it all worth it.

His chest swelled with pride as he listened to his brother using his God-given gift to its full potential. The new version of "Love Triangle" was good. They'd sped up the tempo and added more runs to match the pulsing beat. The kids in the clubs would love it.

He'd hand-carry it to all the DJs at the hottest night spots himself if he had to.

Reggie hit his final riff and the song ended with a bang. Tyler looked through the glass at his little brother and felt a stab of guilt.

He'd decided that Reggie wasn't good enough for Lilah. Who was he kidding? Reggie was a good man with an amazing talent. Any woman would be lucky to have his full attention.

Reggie let the headphones slide down his neck. "So, what did you think, Ty?"

The track was definitely hot, but if Tyler told him that, Reggie wouldn't strive to do better. "It was okay. I'm not sure what, but something was missing. I was hoping for something even funkier, but this should work."

Reggie nodded. "Yeah, it wasn't quite what I wanted, but I thought we needed to get on this sooner rather than later."

Max looked up from his sound board. "I don't

know what you two are talking about. I think this is the jam."

Tyler shrugged. "If this is what you want to go with, we can get Manny to start pushing it out to the clubs."

"No, man, your publicist can only do so much," Max said. "Reg, if you want to get this out, you're going to have to take it to the clubs yourself."

Reggie came out of the recording booth to join them. Tyler clapped him on the back. "All right, kid. If you had to miss dinner Saturday night, I'm glad to see that you put some real work in. This is good work."

Reggie nodded, a small smile curving his lips.

Max laughed. "Damn right we put some real work in. He made me miss a slamming party on the west side. I don't know what he was smoking, calling me at the last minute, insisting we go to the studio, when we already had the time booked for today. I gotta admit though, that extra day made a difference."

Tyler turned and cut his eyes at Reggie. "You called him at the last minute, huh?"

"Look, you just heard the man say that extra day made a difference."

Tyler just shook his head. Reggie never changed.

Reggie grabbed Tyler's arm and pulled him out of the room. "I wanted to talk to you about something."

It was all Tyler could do not to roll his eyes. He was so exasperated with the kid. "What is it?"

"You know how you said the track was missing something? Well, I think so, too. I need to add a different flavor. Maybe a little dirty South to funk it up. I know this guy in Atlanta who works with Jermaine Dupri, and he thinks I could really take my sound to the next level if I spend some time down there."

"And?" Tyler's patience was long gone.

"I was wondering what you thought about that?"

"Let me think about this," he said, without pausing to think at all. "You want to go down to Atlanta where you have almost no contacts, and put your entire music career in someone else's hands? If this guy wants to work with you, let him meet you in the studio here in New York."

"Come on, man, you know it doesn't work like that."

"Do you really think this is the right time for you to play Russian roulette with your music? This time last year, nothing you did could have really hurt you because no one was watching. Now you've got the world's attention. You're on the brink of either hitting it big or disappearing into obscurity. It's up to you, kid."

Tyler turned on his heel and walked back into the room. It boggled his mind that Reggie was ready to blow his whole career on one crazy risk. When was he going to learn that you couldn't have everything overnight? Real success took time.

Reggie did have an amazing talent, but Tyler had been right about him not being ready for a woman like Lilah. Reggie never appreciated the good things that came into his life.

Chapter 10

Wednesday morning, Tyler sat in his office trying to make sense of the last few days. He'd had his hands full with Reggie lately. The kid seemed to be losing a bit of his confidence.

Tyler had thought the blue jeans ad that had come up would have been just what Reggie needed to get his head back in the game. But Manny wouldn't even let Tyler mention it to him. The publicist had said that he couldn't find any information on Hot Pocket Jeans, and he didn't want Reggie getting himself involved with a fly-by-night company.

Tyler had agreed, but he leaned on the guy to get Reggie some kind of promotion to replace it, and Manny had come through with a series of radio interviews that week.

With Reggie finally squared away, Tyler's mind kept wandering back to Lilah. He wanted to see her again, but he didn't know how to go about it without dragging Reggie into the picture.

Suddenly remembering that she had a blog, Tyler opened up his Internet browser. When he'd spotted the address scrawled down the side of her list, he'd instantly committed it to memory. He typed in the address and her most recent entry came into view.

Lilah's List Blog Entry, October 28, 2007

I'm not sure if it's wise to indulge the whims of your youth at the ripe old age of twenty-nine. You see, this is how I ended up with an unusual tattoo in an unusual place.

Tyler continued to read, re-experiencing their tattoo-shop adventure through Lilah's words. He hadn't known that she'd chosen a smiley face for her tattoo because it reminded her of the barrettes she'd worn at the ends of her braids as a child. Or that the happy face was a kind of good-luck charm in her mind because she'd felt especially confident on the days her mother put those barrettes in her hair.

Anyway, I started out this day not wanting a tattoo. What sounds cool at sixteen can seem downright crazy at twenty-nine, right? Maybe not. Even though I was reluctant—and it hurts a lot more than they let on—now that it's over, I'm glad I did it.

~~29. Ride a motorcycle.~~ The same questionable logic applies here. But, let's keep it real—I almost didn't do it.

I was climbing on the back of one of those fancy Japanese Suzkitachithingies, and I had to ask myself…what are you thinking? You barely know this guy. Is he a safe driver? Does he practice good hygiene?

But then I remembered that this guy actually drives his elderly mother home *every night* on this bad boy…so, I had to do it. Whose pride can withstand being a bigger wimp than a seventy-year-old woman?

We drove impossibly fast down some incredibly narrow alleys, and I just knew I would die. The ride was miserable. I didn't enjoy it one bit…until it was over. Then, I felt exhilarated. Alive.

This insane feeling of euphoria has to be why people jump out of airplanes (No, not doing that. Not ever). And, if I'd known I was going to survive the ride, I'm sure I would have loved it.

Suffice it to say, riding on the back of a motorcycle is terrifying—in that roller-coaster sort of way where you scream your head off the entire time, certain of your impending death, then when it's over you want to do it again. Immediately.

Tyler chuckled. Reading Lilah's blog revealed a side to her personality he couldn't have imagined existed. He hadn't realized that she'd been so afraid. He admired her all the more because she'd braved her fears and moved forward.

He was used to the guarded woman who thought twice about every move she made. The woman who wrote this blog was impulsive. She was sassy. He liked the guarded Lilah, but this Lilah intrigued him.

In person, while she readily smiled, she seemed to resist being overly…bubbly. It was almost as if she felt people wouldn't take her seriously if she didn't constantly project a pulled-together image.

Tyler couldn't resist feeling a little bit disappointed at not being mentioned in the blog. After all, he'd been around on her first two days in the city.

He clicked on the Archives link and started reading through her previous entries. Maybe he was mentioned in one of those. Aha! While there were no deep outpourings of her feelings for him, she'd at least referred to him as a hot guy.

While one part of him felt smug in that knowledge. Another part of him felt a bit guilty at gaining free access into Lilah's thoughts. But it was a public forum.

As Tyler clicked back to her home page, he saw that there was a new entry. Lilah must have been logged in at that very moment. He read through her post.

Lilah's List Blog Entry, October 31, 2007

Well, troops, I've had to maintain blog silence over the last few days because there hasn't been any valid List activity to report. I tried to use my stealthy undercover skills for mission directive one: Date Reggie Martin. But I'm sorry to report all attempts have crashed and burned. In the meantime, I'm going to pursue an easy target: ice skating at Rockefeller Center. I haven't been on skates of any kind since I was a teenager, so wish me and my gluteus maximus luck. Over and out.

Tyler found it a bit disturbing to see her infatuation with his brother in writing. He knew that her feelings were superficial, but he felt a twinge nonetheless.

It felt like high school all over again, but now he was the one who had a crush on *Lilah*. Did she have any real interest in Reggie, or was this just something that carried over from high school?

Tyler didn't know, but he'd just been handed an opportunity to find out. If he moved quickly, he could *run into her* at Rockefeller Center.

* * *

Lilah looked down at her watch and rolled her eyes. She'd only been on the ice for fifteen minutes, but it felt like an eternity. All her life she'd watched movies and television shows with romantic moments surrounding ice skating at Rockefeller Center.

Granted, there could only be so much romance when you're skating on your own, but this was one experience that was nowhere near as good as her fantasy.

Lilah showed up in her hat, scarf, gloves and overcoat expecting to enjoy skating on a crisp afternoon. What she hadn't counted on were the hordes of other tourists with the same idea.

The tiny skating center had only one door for entry and exit and standing room only inside. It took her forever to work her way through the throng to pay for a session, then rent skates at one counter and a locker at another.

After exchanging her oversize skates for a pair that wouldn't slide off her feet with each step, she tramped out onto the ice and her feet immediately started hurting. And to top it all off, that particular New York afternoon was unseasonably warm and she was burning up.

Lilah was forced to weave her way through the crowds once again just to put all of her outerwear into her locker. By the time she made it back onto the ice, she was wondering why she hadn't just packed up and left while she'd had the chance.

Placing one foot in front of the other, Lilah made her way around the rink. She was a decent skater. There would be no double-toe loops or triple lutzes, but she could at least make it around without falling. That is, as long as she was able to avoid the moving torpedoes known as children. Lilah was convinced they'd knock her down the way they were recklessly weaving between skaters.

She looked at her watch again. Barely a minute had passed since the last time she'd checked it. Her feet were throbbing, and this experience was anything but fun. Why was she persisting with this torture?

Tyler looked down on the ice at the Rockefeller Center skating rink, searching for Lilah. It only took him a minute to spot her tiny form in a pair of blue jeans and a hot-pink sweater. She was plodding around the rink with a grim expression on her face. She looked like an old lady going twenty-five miles an hour on the freeway, shooting dirty looks at any who dared to pass her.

He felt himself grinning as he watched her. She was all by herself and appeared to be having a miserable time. It was a good thing he'd showed up to surprise her. Hopefully she'd believe his story and he wouldn't look like some kind of stalker.

Tyler paused for a moment. Was he crazy? Was this how stalkers behaved? Then he shook his head. At the first sign that Lilah didn't want him around, he'd leave her alone. But at this point, all the signs showed that she was just as attracted to him as he was to her.

Unfortunately he knew being with him didn't necessarily fit into her current plans. He just had to make her see that plans were meant to be changed.

Just as she was about to head for the exit, a tall figure skated up beside her. "Lilah?"

She turned her head but the man was already moving. He swooped in front of her and began skating backward. Lilah lifted her head and stared up into Tyler Martin's deep brown eyes.

"What are you doing here?" Lilah found herself smiling involuntarily.

"Good afternoon to you, too. I had a meeting at the Rock, and I stopped by to watch the skaters. I couldn't miss you circling the ice like an old lady. I decided to come down here and show you how it's done."

"You were just passing by," Lilah asked, aware that she sounded suspicious.

"Yup." Tyler gazed over his shoulder occasionally, but managed to continue skating backward, weaving through slower skaters with effortless grace.

Lilah shook her head. "How come you're such a good skater?"

Tyler shrugged. "I played hockey for a while in junior high. It's like riding a bike. Your body doesn't forget how to do it once you've learned."

"You're skating backward better than I can skate forward."

"Yeah, the coach made us do drills skating backward. Reggie and I wanted to play hockey after my dad took us to a Capitals game once. He put us into a hockey camp for a few months when we begged to learn to play. We eventually got tired of it. But, like I said, your body never forgets."

Lilah felt a smile curving her lips. *Your body never forgets.* She knew he was referring to skating but for some reason her body had other ideas. Suddenly her body was remembering what it felt like to be pressed up against his body.

She immediately pushed those lascivious thoughts from her mind. But it was difficult because he was wearing a chocolate-brown sweater with brown slacks. He looked fantastic. And to her dismay, some of the mothers watching their children from the sidelines were noticing how good he looked, too.

Just then Tyler leaned forward and took her hands. "You're skating like a senior citizen—like you're afraid of falling and breaking every bone in your body. To really have a good time, you have to accept the fact that you're going to fall. Don't be afraid."

Lilah scoffed. "That's easy for you to say. You look like you were born with those skates on your feet."

"Nonsense. I was watching you. You have good balance. All you need is confidence. Come on, let's go a little faster."

Tyler started pulling her and picking up speed.

"Wait a minute. You can't even see where you're going."

"Sure I can." He glanced over his shoulder and made a last-second correction that swung her out to the left.

Fearing for her safety, she let go of both of his hands and was forced to weave through the other skaters. By this time she was going pretty fast.

And it was suddenly much more fun.

Tyler appeared by her side. "That's what I'm talking about. Keep it up." Then he took off in front of her, weaving around the rink.

Never one to deny her competitive nature, Lilah took that as a challenge. She skated after him without feeling the ache in her feet anymore.

Just as she came up behind him, reaching out to touch the back of his sweater, Tyler would laugh and take off faster, forcing Lilah to pick up speed to catch him.

They played this cat-and-mouse game for a

couple of laps until Tyler suddenly stopped and reversed direction as she reached him. Lilah was going too fast to stop herself, so she tried to take a corner quickly. Out of nowhere a little kid brushed by her and Lilah went down on the ice, hard.

Tyler came to a halt by her side, trying to protect her from the other skaters who might have trampled her.

"Lilah, are you all right?" he asked, pulling her to her feet.

She looked over her shoulder, brushing at the seat of her damp jeans. Then a wicked thought came to her head. "I'm fine. Now you catch me."

And she took off with Tyler in hot pursuit.

Tyler was thrilled with Lilah's quick recovery, and he made short work of catching her. As he came up behind her, he reached out, sliding his arms around her as he pulled her off her feet.

She howled with laughter. And Tyler became immediately aware that he was holding Lilah in his arms.

"No fair," she said when she'd caught her breath. "You're supposed to give me a head start."

He shook his head. "I didn't hear that in the rules. All I heard was, 'catch me.' Now that I have, what's my prize?"

Lilah looked up at him, and for a brief moment

Tyler thought she was going to throw her arms around his neck and plant one on him. At least, that's what he hoped would happen.

Instead she pulled out of his arms as her feet came back to the ice, and they pulled to a halt at the wall.

"Well, I could buy you lunch. I skipped breakfast this morning, and it's just past noon. Do you have time?"

Tyler hid his disappointment behind a grin. "Absolutely. I'm off the rest of the day. It's one of the perks of being the boss."

Of course he'd be up to all hours of the night making up lost time, but it would be worth it. This was the first time since Lilah had come to New York City that he wasn't going to be the third wheel.

Chapter 11

The café Tyler chose was intimate. Lilah felt as though she'd walked into someone's living room. A large fireplace set in the brick wall was the focal point, with a mound of pine-scented wood stacked on the hearth. Scattered about the room were clusters of big armchairs and dainty antique tables. They found a spot near the coffee bar where people lounged with their laptops. The place had a warm homelike feel that Lilah loved.

After discussing the menu and placing their orders, Lilah felt an uncomfortable silence building up. This was the first time that they had truly been alone together. Why did she suddenly feel like she was on a first date?

Lilah searched her brain for something to say. She didn't want to talk about Reggie again. It seemed rude, as if to imply she was only interested in Tyler's company to get closer to his brother. In his position, that probably happened a lot. For her, it may have started out that way, but it certainly wasn't true now.

Tyler had his own attributes. Who knew that he would turn out to be such a beautiful skater? And while Lilah had never envisioned ice skating as a turn-on, it was the way he did it.

On top of that, he was the kind of guy who made her feel like things were under control. He gave off an air of confidence and capability.

Lilah realized that every time the two of them were together, they talked about her and her list. Was there any way to ask him about himself that didn't seem like she was fishing for information about Reggie?

She smiled across the table at him, feeling strangely nervous. After all, they'd already kissed. They weren't exactly strangers.

"Um, when you're not working, what do you do for fun?" Lilah bit her lip, immediately convinced that was a lame question. Before coming to New York, she couldn't have answered that question herself. She'd worked. That was it.

Tyler thought for a moment. "Good question. Being your own boss has its perks, but it also has

its drawbacks. It's hard to know when to quit. I try
to keep to a schedule though." He hesitated again.

"What do I do for fun? Eat out in nice restaurants. On rare occasions, I go to movies. More
often than not, I have to combine my work with
my fun. I see a lot of live music."

"So...you're saying your work is your fun?"

Tyler frowned. "Did I say that? I don't know if
that's quite true."

Lilah studied Tyler's face. He was so different
than she'd remembered him. When she'd known
him years ago, she'd found him intimidating.
Reggie had often complained that he was a self-
righteous do-gooder trying to save the world
single-handedly.

Back then, he'd sat across the kitchen table
from her in Earth Day T-shirts debating liberal
issues.

"You know, I never would have predicted that
you'd get into the entertainment industry. You
always seemed so keen on social work and envi-
ronmental protection," she said.

A pained look crossed Tyler's face, and Lilah
immediately realized her mistake. "Of course, I'm
not trying to imply that your work isn't important.
What you're doing now is exciting and...competi-
tive..."

Had she just fixed things or made them worse?

"No, you're right. I'd always envisioned

becoming a public defender or starting up a legal advocacy group, but that's not where life has led me. I have some volunteer projects that are close to my heart. But there's still so much more I would have liked to do."

Lilah felt her cheeks stinging with embarrassment for putting him on the spot. "I didn't mean to make you feel like—"

He waved her off. "Don't worry about it. It's hard to make the idealism of your youth fit into the reality of adult life. The way I see it, keeping Reggie out of trouble is its own form of altruism."

Lilah didn't know how to respond to that, so she did the safest thing she could think of. She changed the subject. "Speaking of Reggie, what's his schedule looking like for the rest of the week?"

"Reggie's schedule?" Tyler stilled, caught off guard by a sting of jealousy. He'd thought they were starting to connect. And yet, it seemed they couldn't go five minutes without talking about Reggie.

He got a reprieve as the waitress placed a large club sandwich in front of him and a bowl of clam chowder before Lilah.

After the food had been laid out, he answered her question. "This week is pretty hectic for Reggie."

Tyler knew he had to be careful because if he painted Reggie out of the picture entirely, he wouldn't have much reason to see Lilah again. Unless he could get her to acknowledge what was starting to happen between them.

But every time he began to think she was living in the moment with him, he was reminded that her true focus was Reggie.

Of course it was. He was under no delusion that Lilah was here to be with him. She was in New York to complete her list, and dating Reggie was the number-one item. Maybe he should just let them get it over with. Once she saw that she'd be a part of a harem, she might be able to see past Reggie to him.

He couldn't articulate why that mattered so much. Tyler wasn't in the habit of competing with his brother, but this wasn't about winning. It was about getting Lilah to give him a chance.

At that moment the truth of the situation became clear. If he wanted a fair chance, he had to keep Reggie and Lilah apart a little bit longer.

"He's trying to push the remix of 'Love Triangle' in the local clubs right now, and he's doing a lot of radio appearances." Tyler didn't mention that the radio gigs were early morning, and that Reggie wasn't hitting the nightclubs until the weekend. He would still have the next few evenings free.

"Wow, that does sound hectic," Lilah said, gently sipping from her soup spoon. "I'll understand if that means he won't have any time to meet with me. It was a long shot anyway."

Tyler sighed. He hated to see her looking so defeated. "Why don't you let me get back to you on that? Let me see what I can do."

He just wanted these next few days for himself. Once he and Lilah had gotten a chance to spend some one-on-one time together, her meeting with Reggie wouldn't make much difference.

"That's nice of you. But I don't want to make a nuisance of myself."

"Not at all. I love what you're doing with this list. I think it's great to allow yourself this experience. I want to help."

Tyler was struck by the sincerity he felt in that statement. If he kept Lilah and Reggie apart for his own selfish reasons, then Lilah couldn't complete her list. What gave him the right to stand in her way?

"That was so much fun," Lilah said as Tyler walked with her through Times Square toward her hotel. The weather was mild and she enjoyed walking through the city, despite the dense crowds on every sidewalk.

Lilah sucked in a deep breath. Her skin was tingling. She still felt every bit like a woman on a date. No, not a woman. She felt like a teenage girl who somehow managed to get the captain of the football team to walk her home.

It felt good to be in Tyler's company. She really liked him, and they seemed to have a strong chemistry pulling them together, but something was holding her back.

Was it Reggie?

Sure, she'd had a crush on him in high school. He'd represented everything that was unattainable in her life. Yet she and Angie had hatched plan after plan to get his attention to no avail. Even now, when the opportunity was presenting itself again, it seemed she couldn't even get him into the same room.

She honestly didn't have any grand fantasies of meeting Reggie and becoming his girlfriend. After her divorce, Lilah knew she didn't have any business dating anyone. But it would still be nice to look into the face of her high school crush and have him see the woman she'd become. Was she someone he'd take notice of this time?

Since she was going back to her life in D.C. next week, it was unreasonable to start anything with Tyler or Reggie.

But was she leading Tyler on or just living in the moment? Since their exchange of kisses in the nightclub, he hadn't made any overt moves on her. But a woman knew when a man wanted her. And all the signs pointed toward Tyler wanting Lilah.

She should come right out and tell him they shouldn't start something they couldn't finish.

Lilah craned her neck to see Tyler's face. As they turned the corner and began approaching her hotel, she slowed her steps. "Tyler?"

"I've been wanting to tell you something," he started, drowning out her soft inquiry.

Lilah swallowed hard, hoping whatever came next wouldn't be some great profession of devotion that would dampen her upcoming speech. "What is it?"

"Watching you work through your list has made me think about the things in my life that I've always wanted to do."

She felt almost giddy with relief. "Really? Like what?"

"I've always wanted to go to Africa. I've never tried skiing, and I want to become a part of the Big Brother program."

"The reality show?"

"No, the organization Big Brothers Big Sisters. Your list has made me start thinking about the choices I've been making lately."

Lilah couldn't hold back her smile. "That's really cool."

"You've really inspired me, Lilah. You've reminded me that it's never too late to start making changes." They both came to a stop in front of her hotel.

Lilah stared up at Tyler and felt an overwhelm-

ing desire to kiss him. Forgetting her earlier reservations, she stood on her tiptoes and whispered,
"Thank you," just before she pressed her lips to
his.

Chapter 12

Tyler looked out the window of his Park Avenue apartment without really seeing the landscape stretched out before him. The words he'd said to Lilah right before she kissed him echoed in his head.

This wasn't where he'd expected to be at thirty-two. Why was he still a bachelor living alone in a high-priced apartment building? Where was his single-family home? His wife? His kids?

He hadn't spent years in law school to become a managerial advisor to celebrities. He'd wanted to defend the innocent and the needy from those with more power and means.

His original plan had been to join the Peace Corps after law school. Before he started work, he'd hoped to spend some time getting in touch with the true people in need around the world.

It pained him to look around his professionally decorated apartment with state-of-the-art appliances from heated towel racks to a talking stove. The monthly rent was enough to feed a Third World country.

Tyler had tried to console himself over the years with the fact that his brother needed him. He couldn't abandon him now that he was finally getting somewhere in his career. But there was still a little part of him that wondered if his constant support was holding Reggie back.

Maybe the kid would be forced to walk on his own, if Tyler wasn't always there for him to lean on. But Tyler would never be able to forgive himself if his brother drowned because he'd dropped him into the ocean and told him to swim. Maybe there would come a time when Reggie didn't have to rely on him so much, but that was going to have to happen slowly over time.

For now, Tyler had to look for other ways he could make some things happen in his life. He walked over to his computer and opened up a word processing program. At the top he typed, "Tyler's List." And under that he added, "1. Join the Big Brothers program."

As he was adding to his list, the doorbell rang. Tyler was tempted to ignore it. It was too early for Reggie to be popping over. But the doorman would have buzzed him for anyone else, unless...

Tyler pulled open the door. "Monique."

The woman came forward so fast, Tyler was forced to back up hastily.

"Well now, I expected a warmer greeting than that, Ty." Then she wrapped her arms around him and kissed him forcefully.

Tyler tried to extricate himself from the embrace as gently as possible. He hadn't had a date with Monique in almost two weeks.

"Where have you been, *mon cher?* I've been leaving messages ever since I got back from L.A."

"Sorry, Monique. I've been in and out all week. I haven't had time to listen to my messages."

"*C'est la vie,* I've got you here now. Let's make the most of it." She reached down and started pulling up his sweater.

Tyler used to like her aggressiveness, but at the moment it was more annoying than her habit of peppering her speech with French. Her mother was from Montreal but as far as Tyler knew, Monique was full-blooded American.

Pulling away from her grasping hands, Tyler walked across the room, hoping he'd chosen a safe distance. The woman was five-nine barefoot

and today she had on pointed-toed boots that made
her almost even with his height. And Monique
was not only aggressive, she had quite a temper.

"Why are you way over there?"

After spending several days with Lilah, he'd all
but forgotten about Monique. They'd never gotten
beyond a few dinners when she was in town and
her spontaneous late-night visits.

Tall, dark Monique with her short spiky haircut
was the polar opposite of Lilah's gold-and-honey
compact curves. It was almost as if she'd cast a
spell on him. Because ever since Lilah came to
town, Tyler had started to realize that nothing in
his life was as it should be.

"I'm over here because we need to talk."

Monique gave him a hard stare. "Oh, the 'we
need to talk' speech? Really, Ty, aren't we above
that? We're both adults. If you don't want to see
me anymore, just come out and say it."

Tyler eyed her suspiciously. "I don't think we
should see each other anymore."

Monique crossed the room. "See, now wasn't
that easy?" Then she threw her arms around him
and started tugging on his sweater again.

Tyler grabbed her wrists. "What are you
doing?"

"Don't I at least get goodbye sex?"

"No. That's not a good idea, and you know it."

"Nonsense, *mon cher.* All my ideas are good."

She leaned forward to kiss him and Tyler had to duck out of her embrace.

"Monique! I don't think you're hearing me. I've met someone else."

She spun on her heel. "And what does that have to do with me? I've had a very hectic day. I want sex!"

Tyler stopped in his tracks to take in the irony of the moment. He actually had a petulant woman in his apartment, whom he'd just broken up with, begging him for sex like a four-year-old begging for a cookie.

The tension of the moment needed to be released somehow and Tyler couldn't hold back any longer. He started laughing.

Monique's jaw dropped. As Tyler's laughter subsided, he could read the mix of anger and embarrassment on her face. He wondered briefly if his life was in danger.

Then she grabbed her coat and stalked out of the room.

Tyler collapsed onto the couch, weak from his laughter. He couldn't help thinking he'd just dodged a bullet.

He couldn't explain how good that had felt. Breaking up with Monique was the first in a long list of changes he wanted to make.

Next on the list…Lilah.

He had to stop playing the sidekick and flat-out tell her what he wanted. He'd bought himself a little bit of time with her, and he couldn't afford to waste it.

It was time to take her out on a real date.

Thursday morning, Lilah sat in Rick's Café, the guest lounge in her hotel, knitting. She'd chosen a muted blue yarn for her third attempt. Her initial tries at first a sweater and then a blanket had been overambitious. But this time she was going to knit a scarf, and she was determined to complete it, for better or worse.

The trouble was, knitting was so relaxing that her mind tended to wander. And sure enough, before she knew it, she'd blown the pattern and was back at square one. She had to stay focused.

But it wasn't long before her thoughts floated back to Tyler. After all her mental self-talk about not getting involved with him, she'd gone ahead and planted one right on him.

What had she been thinking? She hadn't been. She'd been too busy feeling. Tyler had said he was inspired by *her*. It had been a long time since a man had made her feel good about herself without wanting something in return. She'd been so touched and flattered that kissing him had seemed like the most natural thing in the world.

He'd responded right away. Fortunately they'd come to their senses quickly because they were standing on a busy New York sidewalk. They'd said their goodbyes, and Lilah had gone to her room, wishing he had come with her.

She stared down at the blue yarn in her fingers. Lilah didn't know why she'd chosen that color for a scarf, it wasn't her color at all. But it was a shade that would look wonderful against Tyler's dark skin.

Maybe she should make it a gift for him. Tyler had gotten them past the door at Duvet and had shown her around the city. She should definitely give him the scarf.

She was only going to be in New York a short time, but that didn't mean that she couldn't make the most of it. Lilah hadn't let herself think about it, but there was at least one more item on her list that she could use Tyler's help with.

Lilah felt a hot blush stinging her cheeks. The idea of sleeping with Tyler made her body warm all over. Swallowing hard, Lilah tried to refocus her attention on her knitting. And not a moment too soon because she'd been repeating a crooked stitch and the pattern had become deformed, again.

Trying to fix her mistake and blank her mind with a zenlike focus, Lilah was startled when her cell phone rang.

She picked it up without checking the number, assuming the call was from Angie. "Hello?"

"Lilah, where the hell are you?"

"Chuck?" Lilah was so stunned to hear her ex-husband's voice on the line, all she could do was stare at the phone with her mouth hanging open.

"Where have you been? You don't answer your phone, your car hasn't been moved in days, and no one at your office will tell me where you are."

"That's probably because it's none of your concern, Chuck. We're divorced, remember?"

"That has nothing to do with this. I was worried. How was I supposed to know you weren't hurt or killed?"

Lilah felt her ire rising. She wasn't going to give in to his guilt trips anymore. She'd divorced him so that she'd no longer have to placate his neediness.

"As you can hear, I'm alive and well. Don't call me anymore."

"Are you kidding me? I'm supposed to stop caring about you just because you're no longer my wife."

"You're definitely supposed to stop calling. You're supposed to stop driving by my house to see if my car has moved. And you're supposed to stop harassing my coworkers."

"Wow, and here I thought we could try to be friends."

Lilah was speechless. "Friends? Chuck, I wish

you well. I really do. But I don't think friendship is a reasonable expectation. Move on with your life. I have."

With those parting words, Lilah disconnected the line. Her knitting lay forgotten in her lap as she stared off into space for several minutes.

Finally she gathered up her things and headed toward the elevator. She no longer felt like knitting. And when she did, it certainly wasn't going to be a gift for any man.

Lilah's cell phone started ringing again as she entered her room. She was tempted not to answer it. It was so typical of Chuck to call right back after she'd hung up on him.

One thing was for certain, Lilah was through putting up with this kind of behavior. "Chuck, you've got to stop calling," she said without preamble.

"Uh, Lilah, it's Tyler. Who's Chuck?"

Lilah's heart started hammering. Tyler.

"My ex-husband."

There was a long silence on the line. Tyler probably hadn't known she'd been married. Well, so what? She had been and it was over. Talking to her ex-husband brought back all those intense feelings of unhappiness and frustration.

"Sorry. What can I do for you, Tyler?"

Chuck just reminded her how futile relationships could be. When she'd finally accepted that her marriage was over, she'd felt more relief than grief. Nothing in life should be that hard.

"I was just wondering if you had plans for dinner this evening."

Lilah straightened. "Oh, wow, is Reggie free tonight, after all?"

There was a long pause. "No, Reggie's still on the move. I was wondering if you'd like to have dinner with me."

Lilah swallowed hard, feeling her cheeks heat with embarrassment. "Oh, uh, I was going to say that I hope he's not free because I already have plans. I mean—it would be nice to have dinner with you, too, but… I mean, not 'too,' I would love to have dinner but—"

Lilah couldn't seem to make herself stop rambling.

"That's okay, Lilah, I get it."

"Um, what do you mean? Get what?" Oh no, she'd offended Tyler.

"That you're not free. Have a good evening." He didn't wait for her to say goodbye before disconnecting the line.

Chapter 13

"I cannot believe he had the nerve to call you," Angie stated as they stood on the top deck of the ferry to the Statue of Liberty.

"Just the sound of his voice puts me on edge. We're not even married anymore and he still wants to keep me on a leash. He actually thinks I need his permission to leave town."

Angie threw her arms around Lilah, shrieking, "It's all right. He can't hurt you anymore." Angie's comical theatrics had the desired effect and Lilah burst into laughter.

"Okay, he wasn't abusive, but he was controlling, and I'm still bitter that I put up with it for so long."

"That's why I think you should start dating again. As soon as possible."

Lilah rolled her eyes. "Not this again."

"It's been almost a year and a half. It's time. You shouldn't have blown Tyler off. I know you want to date Reggie, but I say the more the merrier."

It took them several minutes to disembark the ferry, and Lilah had thought their discussion of her nonexistent love life was over. Angie didn't agree.

"I hate to be the bucket of ice water here, but if you don't start dating, or at least pick out a candidate for a serious one-night stand, how are you going to complete everything on The List?"

"Item 38?"

"Exactly."

"I don't need a man for that," Lilah said, unable to hide her blush.

"Girl, that would be no fun at all."

"I'm just joking. I don't know what to do about that. You know me. It's completely unrealistic for me to get that close to someone in the next week."

"Yeah, right. And you've kissed Tyler how many times?"

Lilah looked away. "That doesn't count."

"Tease."

"What?" Lilah stopped in her tracks.

"You heard me," Angie said over her shoulder, forcing Lilah to catch up to her. "You're a tease.

What kind of woman takes every opportunity to fuse her lips to a man's but won't consent to a proper date? You need to face reality. You like Tyler. Tyler likes you. You need a man for item 38."

Lilah blinked at Angie. She knew her friend didn't believe she was a tease, but her blunt words caught her off guard, nonetheless.

"It's not like you'd have to marry him. So…what's the problem?"

Marry him? Was that the problem? Were her feelings for Tyler the kind that led to marriage?

Lilah shook her head. The prospect of it all was just too overwhelming. "I'll tell you what the problem is, Angie. Too much of this trip has been focused on men already. I came to New York to spend some quality time with my best friend. If at the end of my time here, that's all I've accomplished, the journey will be well worth it."

Angie gave her a cherubic smile for a moment. "Aw, that's sweet…but quit trying to change the subject. You're still not completely focused on completing your list. I feel like I'm more committed to getting everything done than you are."

"That's not true. Here we are at the Statue of Liberty. This is something I've always wanted to see in person. Let me enjoy the moment. I'll worry about the next task when this one is done. Here, take my picture."

Despite the density of the crowd milling about the base of the statue, Lilah was able to find a spot that showed her in the foreground and the majestic statue behind her.

Staring up at the famous icon, Lilah was genuinely surprised at how impressed she was. Lady Liberty was so much bigger than she ever could have imagined. And to think this amazing symbol of freedom was a gift.

Lilah looked back over the Hudson River and admired the Manhattan skyline. Lilah thought back to her lonely trip to Ground Zero a few days ago, where the World Trade Center used to stand.

When Lilah had begun making her list fourteen years earlier, she could never have known such a site would exist. She'd grown up thinking if you tried to be a good person and did your best, your reward was that nothing bad would happen to you.

Now, the nearly thirty-year-old Lilah knew the truth. No matter what you do, sometimes bad things happened anyway.

Since that realization, Lilah had continued to play it safe. Trying to mitigate her chances of anything further going wrong.

What good did that really do? As Lilah looked back over her first few days in the city, she realized the people of New York didn't cower inside. They got out each day and lived.

They lived.

If Lilah kept trying to play it safe, what stories would she have to tell her grandchildren? She might have a long life, but it would be a boring one. But if she completed The List, she could die the next day with some brilliant memories and some amazing experiences.

Lilah's List Blog Entry, November 1, 2007

Is it possible to die from public humiliation? In just a few hours I'll be able to tell you firsthand. Of course, that's only if I survive. I'm talking about karaoke, my friends. Lilah Banks appearing for one night only.

Tyler studied Lilah's blog, contemplating his next move. Was it time to bow out gracefully? Lilah had clearly blown him off.

According to her writings, she would be at a karaoke bar that evening. If she'd wanted to, she could have invited him along, or even agreed to have dinner with him before or afterward.

Lilah was definitely sending him mixed messages. But he'd learned some interesting information today. She was divorced. That could have any woman running scared.

How long had she been divorced? If the guy was still calling her, it must have been recent. The last thing he wanted was to start up a rebound relationship. They already had the fact that they lived in separate states working against them.

Tyler just didn't know what to do. He'd never had to work hard to pursue a woman before. He wasn't shy, but he'd found himself dating women who were aggressive and liked to be the pursuers.

He needed some advice. Tyler had many male friends, but at the end of the day, there was really only one person he could confide in.

He picked up the phone and dialed.

"Yo." Reggie answered the phone.

"Hey, man, I know you're probably getting ready to go out tonight. But I need some advice."

"You want *my* advice?" There was a long pause as if he was waiting for a retraction. "Cool, what do you need?"

"I need to know how to get a woman's attention."

"Bro, I love you and all. But I just can't, in good conscience, give you advice about Monique. I still think that chick is a—"

"I know," Tyler cut him off. "Which is why you'll be thrilled to know that I broke up with her. I'm interested in someone else, but she keeps sending me mixed signals."

"Okay, now you're speaking my language. There's nothing like a good challenge to spice things up with a woman. So, you think she's interested, but just when things get going she backs off?"

"She seems fine with being friends, and we've flirted a lot. More than flirted. She's even made the first move a few times. But she doesn't seem to want to acknowledge that there's something developing."

"Hmm. Maybe she just wants to get physical. And if that's the case, bro...I can't see a problem."

"I'm pretty sure it's not that. I found out that she's divorced. I think that may have something to do with it."

"Ah, that's bad news, man. Divorcées come with baggage."

Tyler ran his hand over his head. "So what are you saying? You can't help me?"

"No, I'm not saying that at all. I'm just asking...are you sure you want to get involved?"

"I'm sure. I'd at least like to get a straight answer from her, once and for all. If she doesn't want to be with me, that's fine. But I don't want to give up if she's just scared and needs a little push."

"Okay, you need to make a grand gesture. When I'm at a club and some girl I'm trying to talk to is playing hard to get, I have a foolproof method. This may not work for you, but I usually ask the DJ to get me a mic, and I serenade her in front of everyone. That melts girls like ice in the sun."

Tyler sighed. "You know I can't sing. You hogged all the musical skills."

"Well, you have to find your own mojo, but the key is the grand gesture. Girls like all that white-knight type of stuff. You know?"

"I hear what you're saying, but I don't think I can deliver. This girl and her friend are going to be at a karaoke bar tonight. Trying to sing isn't going to get me anywhere."

"Then you're going to have to make her jealous."

"What?"

"Yeah, turn the tables on her. If there's one sure-fire way to get a girl off the fence, it's another woman."

Tyler rubbed his temple. This was definitely crossing a line. Could he really do something like that? Maybe this thing with Lilah just wasn't meant to be.

"I don't know about that, Reggie. If she sees me with someone else, I could blow my chances with her completely."

"Ty, you know business. I know women. Isn't that why you came to the expert? Here I am giving you full access to all the player skills in my arsenal, but what's the point if you don't have the guts to use them."

"It has nothing to do with guts, it has to do with principles."

"Principles don't keep you warm at night. Aren't you the one who's always telling me that nothing worth having comes easy? Isn't she worth the risk?"

Tyler stared at his feet, exasperated. "It's just not an option. I just told you that I broke up with Monique—"

"Say no more. I don't want you going down that road again. She was too much."

"You can say that again. Can you believe after I broke things off, she literally chased me around the apartment, begging for breakup sex? She was a freak."

"Wait a minute…she was a freak? Do you mean in bed?"

Tyler could practically hear the gears turning in his brother's head. "Don't even think about it. She'd break you in half. Let's get back to my problem."

"Oh yeah. Okay, shaking it off. There's another way to go about this. You stay completely blameless, but it still has the desired effect. Are you game?"

Tyler paused. He wanted Lilah's attention, but was scheming the right way to go about getting it?

He blew out the breath he was holding. Reggie was right, women wanted grand gestures. And Lilah was definitely worth the risk.

"I'm listening…."

Chapter 14

Lilah and Angie stood on the curb in front of the hotel as a battered, old, navy sedan pulled to a stop in front of them.

"I think this was a mistake," Angie whispered.

Lilah nodded. Since the two of them were going downtown for karaoke that night, she'd decided to use the car service Maureen had recommended. Sanjay Mumbari had been polite and friendly on the telephone, so she'd felt pretty good about hiring him to drive them to the bar.

Sanjay bounded around the car to open the door for them, his enthusiasm apparent in the wide toothy smile that glowed against his dark features.

All the two women could do was smile back and climb in.

"Don't you ladies worry. I know this city like the back of my hand. I'll get you to your destination quickly and safely," he said after they were situated in the back seat.

"I'm sure you will," Lilah replied with false optimism. They'd agreed on a flat rate over the phone, so at least she didn't have to worry about getting ripped off. That had to count for something.

"Sanjay, how old is this car?"

"Angie!" Lilah poked her friend.

"It's a 1997 Oldsmobile Cutlass Supreme. I know it's not the height of luxury and style, but it's only temporary."

"I wasn't trying to be rude," Angie was hasty to add. "It's obvious that you keep it very…clean."

"Please don't let the exterior fool you," Sanjay said, the enthusiasm drained from his voice. "Even though it's ten years old, it's in top condition. But if you have concerns, my brother owns Mumbari Limousines. I could give you his number if you don't find this ride satisfactory."

"Sanjay, if your brother owns a car service, how come you don't work for him?" Lilah asked.

"My brother doesn't believe in nepotism. He says I need to make my own way in the world before I have a job in his company handed to me."

"Hmm, if you ask me, that's kind of harsh," Angie said.

"Oh no. This is the only way I know to prove myself to him. I only have one car, and it's not new, but I've invested a lot of time and money replacing parts and making sure it runs smoothly. And I've memorized all the shortcuts and traffic hazards in the city. I promise, what my vehicle lacks in luxury, I will make up for in quality of service. Can I offer you ladies some bottled water?"

Both Angie and Lilah were swayed by Sanjay's earnest attitude. The ride passed safely and smoothly as the three of them chatted. By the end of the journey, Lilah had promised him her exclusive business for the rest of her stay in New York, and Angie had taken a stack of his cards to pass out at the theater where she worked.

"This place is cute," Angie said, leading Lilah into McShanahan's Bar. It was an old Irish pub but the feature attraction was karaoke.

The karaoke platform at the far end of the main room was set up like a concert stage with two large screens for the audience and lots of colorful swirling lights. There was a DJ booth to one side where the singers signed up and chose songs.

It was a much bigger production than the mike stand in a corner that Lilah had been expecting. At that moment a petite blonde and a large Black man were doing their own spirited rendition of "Ebony and Ivory."

Angie started searching for an empty table. It was still early, so the bar wasn't crowded. "This is going to be so much fun. Are you ready for this?"

"Just as soon as we get those appletinis flowing. Thank God you're the only person I know here."

Angie stopped in her tracks, causing Lilah to slam into her back. "I'm not so sure about that."

Lilah looked around Angie to where she was pointing. With a prime seat right in front of the stage sat none other than Tyler Martin. If that wasn't bad enough, he was surrounded by four gorgeous women.

Lilah just stood in the middle of the floor staring. Angie turned around to face her. "Should we go over and say hi? Maybe he needs two more girls to complete his harem."

"No," Lilah said stiffly. "Let's just sit back here."

She parked herself on the nearest chair, at the nearest table, which thankfully was free. They were much farther back in the room, and Tyler would have to turn around to see them because his seat faced the stage.

Angie pulled up a chair. "I still think we should say hello. If Tyler gets up to sing or goes to the bathroom, he'll see us and wonder why we didn't come over."

Lilah's entire body felt numb. "Maybe we should just leave."

"What?"

"There's got to be other karaoke bars. This is New York City."

"Everyone thinks the city has two of everything and they're often wrong. There are probably other places to sing karaoke, but this is *the* karaoke bar in New York. Why are you trying to run anyway? Is it those women? Maybe they're all coworkers or something."

"He's self-employed." Lilah took a deep breath. She had to pull herself together. "Besides, I don't care that he's up there with a bunch of women. I just don't want to sing staring right into his face."

"Okay, we can leave if you really want to, but I think you should just go for it. We're here. You two are just friends, right? You just got finished telling me that you didn't have room in your life for anything more."

Lilah shrugged. When had she become so wishy-washy? She used to be a pretty decisive person. When she wanted something, she'd write it down and she and Angie would hatch out a plan on how to get it.

She'd gotten a number of things in life that way. She was homecoming queen in college because she and Angie, sick of the type of girls who'd won in high school, had launched a campus-wide campaign for votes.

She'd picked Chuck out at a fraternity step show and had decided he was the man for her. She and Angie had spent a lot of time loitering around the poli-sci building until he'd noticed her.

And when she'd wanted a lavish fairy-tale wedding on a shoestring budget, it had taken a year and half of saving, and a lot of ribbon, glue and beads, but she'd made it happen.

Now, here she was, a shadow of her former self, and she was letting her failed marriage rule her life. She was acting as if she owed the world something, instead of just taking what she wanted. The way she used to.

At the moment all she wanted was to sing one song at this karaoke bar. Tomorrow, she wanted to have a small, simple date with Reggie Martin. Why was she waiting for Tyler to set something up? Why didn't she just take what she needed? It was time to cut out the middleman and go get what she wanted.

And after that was done, she would go after what she *really* wanted and enlist Tyler's help with Item 38.

Tyler tried to casually look over his shoulder. Lilah had arrived, and for a minute or two, he was afraid she was going to walk right back out the door. He was starting to worry that this plan was a bit too drastic, but it was too late to turn back now.

"Which one is she? The tall sunflower or the petite yellow rose? No, don't tell me. The rose is definitely more your type."

"Keira, you certainly have a way with words," Tyler said.

Keira Theophilus, gorgeous with her wild curling black hair and olive skin, lived in the apartment across the hall from Tyler, and she ran *The Manhattan Underground,* a weekly lifestyle and culture newspaper for New Yorkers.

She'd been the first to agree to help with Reggie's plan. To set the stage, he'd let Keira read Lilah's blog, and she'd been impressed enough to promise the blog a mention in the next issue of her paper.

Since Tyler hadn't wanted to look like he was on a date, he'd enlisted the help of several female friends as Reggie had suggested.

It had been short notice, and Tyler had been skeptical about finding anyone willing to help. But as soon as he let the girls know he needed assistance winning a woman's heart, it was amazing how quickly they'd all gotten on board.

Rounding out the group of ladies was his accountant, Sarah, an elegant woman with mahogany skin and a close-cropped natural hairstyle, his office assistant, Jenny, a perky twentysomething who'd brought along her hipster friend Christina.

"She's lovely, don't you think?" Sarah asked Jenny.

"I approve. I definitely approve."

"She's cute, but keep in mind, if things don't work out with her, I'm available."

Jenny kicked Christina under the table.

The quartet of women had been feeding him tips all evening to prepare him for this moment.

"Pretend not to notice her right away—"

"—but when you finally do, make sure you look thrilled to see her."

"And compliment her on her hair or her clothes."

"—but not both. That's trying too hard."

Jenny waved at the DJ, who nodded back at her. "I hope you're ready for this, because you're up next."

Jenny was an obsessive planner, and since she'd wanted his singing debut to be timed to perfection, she'd put his name in early and conspired with the DJ to work him in at her cue.

At this point, Tyler wondered if there was anyone in the entire bar that wasn't colluding with him to get Lilah's attention. The best thing about having women on his team was that they really knew how to rally the troops.

As the "Ebony and Ivory" couple clambered off the stage, the DJ called him up. Tyler took a deep breath, suddenly feeling sick to his stomach. Was he really going to do this?

The women at his table whooped and clapped, giving him a boost of confidence. He could feel Lilah's eyes on him, even though he hadn't turned around to see her.

This was it—his grand gesture. If it didn't work, he would wave the white flag.

The first familiar cords of "My Girl" started, and the girls' advice started playing in his head.

Maintain eye contact with her so she knows you're not singing to someone else.

It's not about the singing, it's about the attitude.

With his heart hammering in his chest, Tyler looked out across the room and focused on Lilah. She was staring up at him with a stunned expression on her face.

He took a deep breath and sang the first verse. It came out fairly smoothly and in tune. Okay, maybe this wouldn't be so bad, he thought after making it through the stanza. Feeling more confident, he put a little more power behind the chorus, and his voice cracked on the first note.

So much for the singing, time to kick up the attitude. The women at his table cheered encouragement and Tyler threw his body into it, dancing from side to side and snapping his fingers.

When it was time for the chorus again, he sang at the top of his voice, pointing across the room to Lilah. The audience went nuts, clapping and cheering for him.

Tyler knew his voice was terrible, but as he stood on stage with the crowd cheering him on the more he messed up, he got a bit of insight into his brother's world. This was what it felt like to be adored by strangers. No wonder Reggie was addicted to it.

Tyler sang right at Lilah, watching Angie clapping and punching her friend in the shoulder. Lilah stared back at him with a shy, goofy smile, looking helpless to hide her pleasure.

Tyler knew he had her then, so he went in for the big finish. Microphone in hand, he started making his way down from the stage to the back of the room. As he passed through the crowd, everyone stood, a few people clapped him on the back for encouragement.

When he was in front of Lilah, he sank to one knee and sang the last verse. "My gir-rl!"

After returning the microphone to its stand, Tyler came back to Lilah's table and pulled up a chair. "When you said you had plans tonight, I had no idea that you'd be here, too."

"I'm just glad we got here just in time for your performance. You were great," Angie said.

"And you must be deaf," Tyler said, laughing.

"Well, you displayed great showmanship."

"As you can see, Reggie got all the musical

skills in the family. There was nothing left for me. I did that on a dare. I must admit though, when I saw you in the crowd, I got motivated."

Lilah giggled, feeling foolish without really knowing why. "You definitely entertained us. And your friends... It was a great idea to bring your own cheering section."

Lilah hoped her statement wasn't too obvious. She wanted to know who all those women were, but she didn't want to sound jealous.

He couldn't have been dating any of them, because he hadn't been shy about focusing his affections on her. He was clearly making a move. He'd called to ask her out on a date. And now, he just finished singing to her.

"Yeah, can you believe it? Somehow I ended up tagging along on my neighbor's girls' night out. When she asked me to come out with her friends, I had no idea I'd be the only guy."

"Lucky you." Lilah punched his arm playfully, noting the hard muscles underneath his sleeve.

"Yeah? Well, you're the one I really wanted to spend the evening with. Looks like fate wanted us to spend it together, too. Here we are."

Angie muttered something under her breath about being a third wheel and got up. Lilah didn't look up, she was already lost in Tyler's eyes.

"After that performance, how can I go up there? The crowd will boo me off the stage."

"Did you hear my singing? It was awful."

"Not awful, but even if every note wasn't on key, you certainly won over the audience."

"Look at you. All you have to do is flash that sweet smile and they'll be eating out of the palm of your hand. You just have to commit to it."

Before Lilah could answer, her name was called out. "Wait a minute. I didn't even sign up for a song yet." She looked over at the DJ booth and Angie waved back at her.

"Oh no."

"Get up there," Tyler said.

Lilah reluctantly got up from her seat and started for the stage. As she passed the DJ and Angie, she called out, "What am I singing?"

Angie just grinned wickedly. "You'll see."

Lilah took the stage and she heard the first strains of "Nasty Girl," an eighties song by Vanity 6, start playing.

Lilah could feel the heat racing up her neck to her face. This was by no means the type of song she would have chosen for herself. But she was on stage now, the song was gearing up. She had only one choice.

Sing!

Lilah was a terrible friend. While Angie was on stage singing her heart out, Lilah couldn't pull her attention away from Tyler.

During her own performance, Lilah wouldn't have made it through the embarrassment without Tyler's encouragement. He and his friends stood right in front, cheering her on. Inspired by his own fearless performance, Lilah had closed her eyes and pretended she was singing every lyric to him.

And they were provocative lyrics. Now, sitting across from him, they were still all she could think about.

He looked handsome in a dark blue sweater and jeans that hugged his muscular thighs. Even from across the table, she could smell the cologne that she'd begun to identify with him.

It would be so nice to... Wait, before she indulged that train of thought, she had some business to take care of. She had to take contacting Reggie into her own hands. If she crossed off her primary list item, it might actually give her confidence to take care of some of the other more daring things.

"Tyler, can I ask you a favor?"

He smiled at her, showing his gorgeous straight white teeth. "You can ask me anything."

"Do you think you could give me Reggie's cell phone number?"

Tyler blanched. It was truly rare to see all the color drain from a Black man's face.

"I know that sounds presumptuous. But we did

go to high school together, so it's not like I'm a complete stranger. I was just thinking, he obviously wasn't moved hearing of my situation secondhand. Maybe if I could plead my own case, I might be able to convince him...."

She let her words trail off, watching the tension in Tyler's face. Had she upset him? His lips were tight and she could see a vain pulsing at his temple.

Tyler took a long swig from the beer bottle in front of him and regained his composure. "I'm sure you could have him wrapped around your little finger with just a few words," he bit out.

"I'm not saying that. It's just—"

"No, it's true. I remember when you were in school, my brother came in late from track and wanted to blow off the tutoring session. You managed to make him feel like his entire future depended on his spending as much time with you as possible. That was very clever."

Lilah paused, unsure whether or not that was a compliment. "I wasn't trying to be clever. I just wanted—"

"Reggie's schedule is crazy this week. Even though you're a friend, as his business manager, I just can't give out his number without his consent. Let me call him now and ask him."

Tyler stood and walked in the direction of the bathrooms, dialing numbers on his cell phone.

Reggie was still first on Lilah's mind. It was getting harder to hide his exasperation with that fact. Maybe she needed to see Reggie just to remind her what he's really like.

"Yo."

"Reggie, I need—"

"Tyler! How did it go with the mystery girl?"

Before they'd hung up earlier, Reggie had begun to ask questions about the woman for whom Tyler was going to such great lengths. He'd rushed off the phone without giving his brother a straight answer. But now his interest was piqued. How would Tyler explain that Reggie's high school tutor was his mystery woman?

He rubbed his temple. Suddenly the entire scenario seemed to be snowballing out of control. This wasn't going to work. He couldn't ask Reggie to meet Lilah yet. He needed more time to straighten this out.

"Things are going fine. I was just wondering what you were up to."

Reggie laughed into the phone. "Your evening can't be going that well, bro, if you're wondering what I'm doing. Do you need a wingman?"

"No. Your plan worked perfectly. We're all having a great time."

"Glad to hear it. But there's no reason to let all those women go to waste. Where are you? Because I can—"

"Don't worry. Everything's under control. I'll call you later."

When Tyler hung up, he felt lower than the sawdust beneath his feet. What was he doing? Reggie had actually wanted to come join them. That would have made Lilah's night.

He should have let his brother come. Things were already too complicated.

Hitting redial on his cell phone, Tyler asked Reggie to meet them for drinks tomorrow night. This time, when he hung up, he felt much better. Without Reggie standing between them, Tyler would finally be able to get close to Lilah.

Chapter 15

Angie yawned, resting her head on her folded arms. "I'm so tired. Girl, I don't know if I can take another late night like the last one."

They'd closed down the karaoke bar last night, and tonight the two of them were sitting in a country-western bar waiting for Reggie and Tyler. Lilah planned to ride the mechanical bull, but she'd promised to wait for Tyler to show up.

She no longer cared about having a date with Reggie. She'd decided being in the same room with him would be good enough to satisfy her list requirements. Then she'd be able to focus on Tyler.

He was more her type and the chemistry was starting to bubble over between them.

"You could have stayed home tonight, Ang. I can handle two men and a mechanical bull on my own."

Angie snorted. "You really think he'll show?"

"Who, Reggie?"

"Yeah, isn't this, like…the third time he was supposed to meet up with us?"

"He's a celebrity. His schedule is hectic."

Angie propped her head on her palm. "Yeah, I guess."

"What? Are you implying something?" Lilah rubbed her bare arms, wishing she'd worn a sweater with her T-shirt.

"No, it's just hard to believe it's finally going to happen. I mean, all this trouble for a guy we had free access to in high school."

"Yeah. Now that you mention it, he was pretty flaky in high school, too. Always late. Tyler reminded me yesterday how I used to have to talk Reggie into studying when he finally got home."

"Tyler reminded you, huh?"

Once again Angie's tone was loaded. "What does that mean?"

"I don't know. I was just thinking about the fact that he's clearly into you."

"So?" Lilah started chewing on her lower lip.

"And he probably doesn't like it that you're so

hot to date his brother. That seems like a conflict of interest to me."

Lilah sat up straight. "Are you saying you think he never told Reggie about me?"

"No, I'm not saying that at all. I'm just pointing out that it's probably not great for the guy that wants to date you to be your matchmaker."

"Tyler knows I don't expect a real date with Reggie. It's just for The List."

"Does he? He knows you used to have a pretty severe crush on Reggie in high school. Maybe he's worried that the fires will rekindle once you see him again."

Lilah felt her face flush. For reasons she couldn't quite rationalize, she felt like a fool. "Tyler isn't as petty or insecure as you're making him out to be."

Angie waved her off. "I'm not making him out to be anything. Tyler's a great guy. I really like him. I was just pointing out how weird this must be for him, that's all."

"Right, but this whole list thing is weird in the first place. Tyler understands. You'll see."

"Uh, huh," Angie said with an I-told-you-so tone. "Here he is now. Alone."

Lilah turned her head and saw Tyler headed for their table in the honky-tonk bar. "Maybe Reggie is meeting him here," she said, but her stomach was already sinking.

Tyler didn't waste his time with pleasantries as he reached the table. "Is he here yet?"

"Reggie?"

"Yeah, he's supposed to meet us."

Lilah sighed, unable to hide her lack of confidence in that statement.

Tyler looked a bit agitated himself. "Hold on." He took out his cell phone and started dialing.

"Where are you?"

Lilah could only hear Tyler's side of the conversation, and it wasn't looking good. "You've got to be kidding.... You're killing me.... Do you understand how foolish I look right now?... Fine."

Tyler snapped the cell phone closed and turned sheepish eyes on them. "Once again, I'm sorry. He's still at WRQX taping promos."

Lilah rolled her eyes. "Whatever."

Tyler pulled out the chair beside her and sat down. "I know you're disappointed. But you're not mad at me, are you?"

Lilah threw her hands up in defeat. "It's just funny, that's all. Angie and I were just talking about this."

"About what?" he asked, looking back and forth at the two of them.

"About whether or not Reggie would show up this time. And if it was in your best interest to ask him."

"How can you say that? You just heard me talking to him."

"I heard you talking to somebody."

Tyler stared at her. "Are you serious?"

"Look, I'm not calling you a liar. I'm just saying that three strikes and you're out. I'm going to have to think of some other way to get in touch with Reggie."

Once again Tyler looked from Lilah to Angie. "Did you put this idea in her head?"

Angie shrugged. "I just said it may be a conflict of interest. If you really wanted to help her, as Reggie's brother, you probably could have by now."

Tyler sighed heavily. "Lilah, I know you're upset, so I'm going to try not to take this personally. Especially since I thought there was more between us than just my connection to Reggie. All day long I deal with people who want to use me to get to my brother. I thought we had a relationship of our own."

"I'm going let you two work this out," Angie said in a tiny voice, and rose from the table.

Lilah felt her face flame. "Are you saying that I'm using you? You know that's not true. You offered to help me and I accepted."

"Think, Lilah. You know from personal experience how Reggie can be. If it doesn't directly relate to his music career, he flakes out. It's just the way he is. It's the way he's *always* been."

Lilah felt her ire subsiding. She sighed. "Yes, I

know you're right. I'm sorry. I didn't mean to make you feel used. That's the last thing I wanted to do."

Tyler nodded. "Good. Can we still try to have a good time?" He paused to look around. "This is a far cry from where we were last night."

Country music was blaring over the loudspeakers. The main room was dimly lit with lots of dark wood bar stools and booths. The walls were covered with wagon wheels, steer heads and pictures of cowboys and horses.

"Where's the mechanical bull?"

"The bartender said it's downstairs. He says a crowd doesn't form down there until later on."

Tyler sat back. "Okay, then what are you waiting for?"

"Just you." She flashed him her best smile.

Angie came back to the table with a pitcher of beer and three mugs. "Have we cleared the war zone, or should I have brought reinforcements?"

"That bad, huh?" Tyler asked. "I'm sorry about the conflict. My brother was never punctual, but now that he's becoming famous, he's a frequent no-show."

"After hearing you sing last night, I think you might be a rising star yourself. Remember we knew you when," Angie teased.

Lilah looked up from her beer and saw Tyler watching her. "What?"

"I just never figured you for a beer kind of girl."

"Oh really? What kind of girl do I look like?"

As Tyler's eyes raked over her, she felt a bit self-conscious in her tight blue jeans and her I Heart New York baby-T. She hadn't wanted to overdress for bull-riding.

"I had you pegged for white wine spritzer or, of course, an appletini kind of girl."

Lilah smiled. "That's just one side of me. You haven't seen the rest."

As soon as the words were out of her mouth, Lilah heard the double entendre. Tyler's face lit up like a Christmas tree and Angie rolled her eyes.

Lilah shrugged it off. She'd worry about the rest of The List later, for tonight, all she could think about was Tyler.

As he stood among the crowd, waiting for Lilah to climb on the mechanical bull, Tyler couldn't tamp down his warring emotions.

On one hand, he'd gotten what he wanted. He now knew for certain that Lilah wanted *him*. The chemistry between them tonight was explosive.

But on the other hand, he was wrestling a niggling of guilt. She'd called him out tonight. She thought he might have been interfering with her meeting his brother, and she'd been right. Never mind that on this particular occasion, he'd actually tried his best to get Reggie to come.

If he wanted a clean slate with Lilah, he was going to have to explain himself. But what were the right words? Words that would show how much he cared for her without seeming selfish?

There weren't any words like that. Not yet. He needed more time. If she was falling for him the way he'd been falling for her, then she might be able to understand. Perhaps she'd even be flattered.

Tyler shook his head at that notion, but before he could engage in another round of self-flagellation, Lilah was on the bull.

He felt a bubble of laughter burst forth at the sight of her straddling the saddle and gripping the handle with one hand. She looked adorable.

As the mechanical bull started up, making increasingly faster motions, Tyler expected Lilah to fly right off.

Instead he watched as her brow knit with concentration and she tightened her thigh muscles to grip the saddle. Her body jolted violently, but she held tight, undulating her hips to stay seated.

The crowd cheered her on. Some men in the audience shouted lewd remarks regarding her riding skills. But Tyler barely heard them, because his jeans had become uncomfortably tight.

The mechanical bull continued to speed up and Lilah slid off one side onto the foam flooring. She landed smack on her curvy rump. The whole process, from start to finish, took less than a minute.

But the scene was stamped in Tyler's memory like an erotic fantasy.

As she approached him afterward, he could see in her eyes that she knew what he was thinking.

"How did I do?"

Tyler tried not to leer. "I'm impressed. You had a good grip on that bull, didn't you?"

Lilah smiled. "It must be all the yoga. It strengthens the core. I have really good balance."

"I can see that." Tyler had to bite his tongue on the suggestive comments swirling in his head. His whole body had gone hot, and he didn't really care that they were in a crowded room.

He reached out and slid his arm around her waist, pulling her against him. Before he could close in for the kiss, the crowd started whooping again.

Lilah spun out of his grasp and around to face the ring. "We're going to miss Angie's ride."

As Lilah leaned against the rail in front of her to watch her friend, Tyler lined up behind her, resting his chin on top of her head.

His arousal fit right into the small of her back. Lilah reached back to grip his thigh, while he stroked her hair, occasionally brushing the soft skin of her neck.

Even through the cacophony of the rowdy onlookers, Tyler could hear her soft sigh of pleasure. He mentally reviewed his options.

What was the most polite way to get rid of Angie and bring the night to a close? He hoped Lilah was on the same page, because before long he'd be done with the foreplay.

The tension mounting between them for the last few days had reached nearly uncontrollable proportions in the last few hours.

He was only human and Tyler intended to take Lilah home with him this night.

Chapter 16

Later that night Lilah sat with her thigh glued to Tyler's in the Diamond Diner. They'd called Sanjay to pick them up, but Angie had refused to be dropped off until she got a short stack of buttermilk pancakes.

With her nerves rattling inside her like a tambourine, Lilah didn't mind stopping for food, but she could feel the tension rolling off Tyler's body like giant ocean waves.

Sanjay had only been too happy to join them at the table. Now, he was busy scarfing down the biggest plate of food Lilah had ever seen such a skinny man eat.

Halfway through their meal, Remy showed up to wait for his mother and had invited himself to join them. He'd wedged his large body into the booth on the end next to Angie. Now Belle was sliding in next to Sanjay, who was next to Tyler. That pushed Lilah around the big curve in the center of the booth, packing them in tighter than sardines.

"Mechanical bulls sound scary, but I wouldn't have minded the karaoke," Belle was saying. "I love to sing in church every Sunday morning. If only I could get Remy to join me. The good Lord probably wouldn't even recognize him after all this time," she said, shooting her son a reproachful look.

Remy just rolled his eyes. "Speaking of singing, Mama. Do you know who Tyler's brother is?"

"I'm hoping you're going to tell me he's that fine Ludacris."

Angie laughed. "Do you like rap music, Belle?"

Belle nodded. "I like gospel. I'm a little bit country, and I'm a little bit rock and roll. But I like shaking my booty the best."

"My brother Reggie is a far cry from a booty-shaker."

"You know Reggie Martin, Mama. He sings that song 'Love Triangle' that you like."

Belle clapped her hands and launched into the chorus of the song. Then she turned to Tyler. "When you gon' bring that boy 'round here? I want to meet him."

Lilah poked him in the ribs. "Yeah, when?"

Angie chimed in, "Maybe we can all see him at Lilah's birthday party a week from tomorrow."

"It's your birthday, child?"

"How old will you be?"

"Hush, Remy, you don't ask a woman her age."

"I don't mind. I'm going to be thirty. That's why I'm rushing around the city trying to get my list completed. The party's not a big deal. The people at this table are pretty much the only people I know in the city, anyway."

"Oh, don't let her fool you. It's going to be a big deal, and she knows it. The List stipulates that we throw a *wild* party," Angie said.

"Anyway," Lilah said, "whatever it turns out to be, you all are welcome to join us."

"Even me?" Sanjay asked, looking up from his plate with a mouthful of strawberry-covered waffles.

"Especially you, Sanjay," Lilah answered.

"Partying, that's Remy's specialty, but I'm sure you don't want an old woman ruining your good time."

"Nonsense, Belle, you'd be the life of the party." To Remy, Lilah said, "You won't get past the door without Belle. Is that clear?"

"Yes."

Tyler made a big show of yawning and stretching. "It's about that time, guys, don't you think?"

His plate cleaned, Sanjay wiped his mouth and stood. "I'll go pull the car around."

Remy gave Tyler a knowing smile. "Brother, you've been late for the door all night. A little anxious to get to bed?"

Angie snorted. "That's an understatement. These two have been undressing each other with their eyes for hours. I can't wait for them to finally do the deed, so we can all move on."

Belle pretended to cover her ears. "I've got to get these old bones back to work." Then she turned back to Lilah. "But, honey, get a little for me. I'm so old I don't remember what it's like. Enjoy him. That's what they're for."

Lilah covered her burning cheeks with her hands. "I don't know what any of you are talking about."

Angie pushed Remy out of the booth so she could get out. "I'm going to put you two out of your misery and catch a cab back to my apartment. You two can ride in the back of Sanjay's car all by yourselves." She turned to Lilah. "Now, you be a good girl and don't come home until you've gotten l—"

"Don't you dare say it."

Remy shrugged. "I need to smoke a cigarette, anyway. Good night, y'all."

Lilah found herself alone with Tyler for the first time since they'd left the country-western bar.

She turned to look at him. "Can you believe them?"

Tyler stared back at her, his eyes intense. "No, I can't. What the hell took them so long to leave?"

Lilah burst into a bout of nervous laughter. Were they really going to do this? It had been hanging in the air between them all night. But now that they'd finally been left alone, it all seemed surreal.

Tyler reached out and picked up her hand. "Are you ready to leave?"

Lilah took a deep breath. "Yes. I guess so."

"Your place or mine?"

Lilah smiled shyly. "Yours."

Lilah and Tyler barely spoke on the ride to his apartment. When they arrived, she was a bit surprised that he lived in such a fancy place. The opulence and high security of Park View Apartments served as a reminder to what different lifestyles they were living.

When he opened the door, Lilah saw that he lived with all the modern comforts. It wasn't especially warm or inviting. Instead it screamed interior designer. The room was an austere white accented with blues and greens. There were abstract paintings and funky sculptures. Absolutely nothing that reminded her of Tyler.

What did she really know about him anyway? Lilah was starting to have all kinds of second thoughts, and it must have shown on her face because Tyler steered her toward the sofa. "Relax, you look like you're about to face a firing squad."

"No, of course not," she answered, not wanting to offend him. "But I'm not sure this was a good idea. I don't normally have one-night stands."

Tyler eased her back against the suede cushions. "What makes you think this is going to be a one-night stand?"

She popped upright. "You live here. I live in D.C. What else could it be?"

He laid her back again. "We've got more than one night to find out."

Before she could resist, Tyler leaned over her and covered her lips with his. Lilah thought she knew what it was to kiss Tyler. But this kiss was nothing like the foggy kisses they shared at Duvet or the impulsive peck in front of her hotel.

This kiss was deliberate. Both ardent and relaxed. Tyler kissed her as though he had all the time in the world and he intended to savor every moment. While his soft lips parted to allow his tongue to find hers, one hand went to her waist and the other cupped her neck.

Lilah knew there was an army of protests lining up in her head, but it was becoming increasingly difficult to think of them.

Sensation took over. The familiar scent of his cologne that she'd come to find arousing. The texture of his fingertips sliding underneath her T-shirt. A tingling heat had started growing at her core, dominating all the other sensations.

Sinking back into the cushions, she locked her arms around his neck, wishing she could feel the rest of his hard-muscled body against hers.

Letting a small whimper escape her lips, she slid to one side, tugging at his shoulders. Tyler instantly knew what she wanted. He levered his weight off her body, positioning her lengthwise on the sofa, then he lowered himself over her.

Lilah inched her legs around his waist, bringing him up hard against her. That was better, but it still wasn't enough. The ache was growing stronger.

Tyler continued to kiss her, letting his mouth trail from her lips to her neck. She arched against him.

Lilah tugged at his sweater, feeling like a two-year-old without the words to communicate her need. "Off."

Tyler pulled away long enough to strip the sweater and the T-shirt beneath it over his head, revealing a hard, well-muscled chest.

Lilah felt a smile of pure delight curve her cheeks. She ran her hands over the masculine ridges, unable to believe her good fortune.

Tyler's eyes slid halfway closed as he reveled in her touch. "My turn."

He reached down and gathered her up, helping her off with her T-shirt. Her bra was not far behind.

"Yes," he whispered once he'd freed her breasts.

Suddenly, Lilah wondered how she'd gone so long without being touched this way. In that moment she felt as if she'd never been touched like this before.

Her skin burned with every light, feathery caress he trailed along her skin.

In a rush of movement, Tyler scooped her off the sofa and lifted her into his arms.

"Where?"

"We need more room for this," he said, stalking toward his bedroom.

He gently placed her on the bed and then he disappeared. The lights in the room came on, and Lilah was so glad.

She lifted her head just in time to see Tyler unbuckling his belt and stripping off his jeans. He wore red boxer briefs, and those followed the rest of his clothing to the floor.

When he was nude, Lilah reached out for him, and he lowered himself into her arms. But he didn't stay there long as he began removing her clothes.

He pulled off her boots and socks, then her jeans and underwear.

This was normally the point where Lilah began to feel self-conscious, but the look in Tyler's eyes surprised her. He stared, openly soaking her up from head to toe.

His heavy-lidded hot gaze made her feel beautiful and sexy in a way that words never could.

Feeling uncharacteristically bold, Lilah pushed Tyler back on the bed and climbed atop him. He squirmed, trying to touch her, but she commanded, "Be still."

And he did. He lay back while she ran her fingers over his beautiful brown skin. She marveled at the contrast between her lightness and his darkness.

She nipped at his nipples with her teeth, causing him to inhale deeply. She let her tongue flick at his belly button and then she let her mouth go lower.

Tyler immediately groaned with pleasure as her lips found him. His reaction emboldened her and she continued until he grabbed her arms and pulled her up.

In one swift motion he flipped her onto her back. He buried his face in her neck as his fingers readied her for his entry.

Lilah felt so ready for him she almost went over the edge before he could enter her. "Now," she pleaded.

Raising himself on one arm, Tyler entered her slowly, inch by inch. Lilah was filled, feeling a moment of discomfort before he began to move.

She forgot about everything else and she clung to him as he rode her to their mutual completion.

Chapter 17

Tyler awoke to the sensation of being watched. His eyes popped open and he found Lilah's face mere inches from his own.

"Good morning," she said, dropping her lips down on his.

"Good morning," Tyler mumbled against her mouth. This was not a bad way to start the morning. Lately he'd been dating career women, who were always on the go. The type that had to schedule him on their PDAs if they stayed for breakfast.

He propped himself up on one elbow, reaching over to brush her hair out of her face. "Did you sleep well?"

"Yes," she murmured absently. Her hands immediately went to her head. "I must look like a mess."

The curls were gone and her hair hung around her face in a frizzy tangle. "You look adorable."

She continued to feel around, blindly smoothing the tangled mess. "I can tell that's not true. You've just identified yourself as a liar," she laughed, slipping out of bed.

She grabbed his robe that was thrown across an armchair beside his bed and put it on. She was immediately swallowed up in the terry-cloth folds. "I'll be right back."

She disappeared into the living room and returned with her purse, which she took into the bathroom.

As he watched the bathroom door close behind her, Tyler once again wrestled with his emotions. It was wonderful waking up with Lilah in his bed. He'd love to make a habit of it. But part of him felt as though he'd gotten her there under false pretenses.

She'd just called him a liar. She'd been joking, of course, but only because she didn't know any different.

The only way to spare himself the full weight of her disappointment was to confess. When she came out of the bathroom he'd tell her that he hadn't done all that he could to fix her up with Reggie because he wanted her to himself. Would she find that charming or manipulative?

Tyler shook his head. It had to be love. Why

else would he have done something so inexplicably foolish?

He'd tell her the truth, but it would take all his skills as a lawyer to make it sound charming. That was the plan. A confession. As soon as she came from the bathroom.

A few minutes later Lilah came into the bedroom with her hair neatly smoothed to her head. She slipped out of his robe and placed it back on the chair.

"There," she said, pulling back the covers. "We'll just pretend that I woke up this way. Smooth hair and minty-fresh breath."

She covered his naked body with hers and planted a long slow kiss on him. It was a long time before Tyler remembered that he was supposed to be confessing.

Much later that morning, Lilah had gotten out of bed to take a shower and Tyler heard the doorbell ring. Jumping into a pair of jeans and a T-shirt, he ran to the door.

There were only two people who could get up to his apartment without out having to be buzzed in. He made a mental note to tell Nick, the doorman, to take Monique off the list. She wouldn't be making any more late-night visits.

The other person was his brother. Nick was a huge fan and was more than willing to lay down the red carpet for Reggie.

In this moment Tyler wouldn't be too happy to see either visitor. He was still contemplating which scenario would be worse when he peeked through the peephole and saw Reggie.

If he ignored the doorbell, his brother would only become more persistent. Tyler tried to open the door a crack. "Hey, man, what's up?"

Reggie pushed the door and burst into the apartment. "We've got to get some money together for a tour or something. I need to build more name recognition."

"Uh, okay…let's sit down with the team and go over our options next week."

"Uh, okay? Okay? Is that all you have to say? Last night was a disaster, man. Since the radio promos ran long, I didn't get a chance to meet up with Manny, so the bouncers at Clue wouldn't even let me in. They didn't care that I had a scheduled appearance."

Tyler barely heard what Reggie was saying over the rapid pounding of his heart. If Lilah came into the living room right then, he'd be completely busted. It wouldn't take long for Lilah to realize Tyler had been keeping them apart. He'd already planned to confess. If he hadn't let himself get distracted, he wouldn't be at risk of looking like a complete jerk at the moment.

"No, not okay just like that. I just don't think this is the right time or place to discuss this."

"What? You've got something better to do?"

Tyler couldn't stop himself from looking over his shoulder toward the bedroom.

"Ah, I get it. You've got someone better to do."

"Um…yeah, so as you can see it would be best if you leave."

Reggie started toward the bedroom. "No way, I've got to see the girl who has you running around in circles."

"She's in the shower, and if you take one more step, I'm going to take you down."

"What's the big deal? Yesterday you wanted me to meet her."

"Well, today she's naked, so the offer is off the table. Please leave."

"Fine, but first I have to pee." Reggie ducked into the guest bathroom before Tyler could stop him.

Tyler turned toward the bedroom, noting with some trepidation that the shower was no longer running. Just then Lilah walked out with nothing but a large bath towel wrapped around her.

"I was wondering if you have something I can throw on," she asked.

"You don't need any clothes. Just go climb back into bed."

"But I thought we were going to eat."

"Yes, in bed. It's on your list. Spend an entire day in bed. Go on, I'll bring you the food once it's ready."

Tyler had just closed the bedroom door behind Lilah when Reggie came out of the bathroom in the hallway.

Tyler grabbed him and started ushering him to the front door. "My lady friend was just out here in nothing but a towel. You've got to get gone. Now!"

"Jeez, you're rude. This better be some hot chick because—"

Tyler closed the door in Reggie's face. He'd have to make it up to his brother later. Once he'd set things right with Lilah.

He sucked oxygen into his lungs, hoping now his heartbeat would finally go back to normal. He just wasn't cut out for deception.

As the door closed in Reggie's face, he couldn't help noticing the metaphorical parallel with his music career. He'd come over here today, expecting his brother to help him like he always did.

Instead he'd gotten the bum's rush. Just the way he'd gotten it in the club last night.

At first he'd thought he was on top of the world. That it would be easy street from here on out. Nothing but fancy cars, designer clothes and Cristal champagne dripping from the faucets. His first single had been well received.

He'd started getting recognized on the street and VIP treatment around town. Now that his album had dropped, the critics had changed their tune. They still liked his voice, but now they claimed he had too many ballads to hold the attention of his younger target audience.

He still received some celebrity perks, but now, more than ever, it was becoming clear that they were B-list perks. He wanted to be on the A-list.

Reggie was starting to see that it was going to take a lot more than one hit single to get him where he wanted to be. He'd thought Tyler would always have his back, but it was starting to look like he was on his own.

If he wanted to get his career to the next level, he was going to have to take some chances.

Lilah lay back against the pillows in Tyler's bed as he cleared away their dishes. She couldn't remember the last time she'd felt so pampered.

When she'd added *spend the entire day in bed* to her list, she'd been in high school. She'd been resentful of the days she had to get up early to go to school and the weekends that she had to do chores and family bonding activities.

At the time, she'd looked ahead to being an adult who could spend her time as she chose. And in her sixteen-year-old mind that had meant never changing out of her pajamas, watching old movies and eating cereal all day.

When Tyler had told her that this was to be her

day in bed, it instantly took on a much more decadent connotation.

She was presently wearing only his T-shirt, and he wore a pair of boxer briefs. The thought of spending the afternoon in his fluffy, downy sheets made her happy. Inside the cocoon of his apartment, time seemed to stand still.

Tyler came back from the kitchen and climbed into bed next to her. "I figure for this to qualify as spending the entire day in bed, we have to camp out here, eat all our meals and entertain ourselves here, right?"

"I guess so, but I don't want you to feel roped into this. You must have had other plans for today."

"I can't think of a better way to spend a Saturday. I'm looking forward to it, in fact."

Lilah laughed. "I'll just bet you are."

Tyler laughed, too. "Let me see that list of yours. I want to see how much progress you've made."

Lilah found her purse and pulled out her hard copy, which was sometimes handier than her PDA version.

Tyler studied The List carefully. Finally he looked up at her. "All of the stuff you have crossed out are things you've already done?"

Lilah nodded.

"You've read all the works of Shakespeare?"

"Yeah, that was one of those things that

sounded good on paper, but ended up being a real drag. I started off really excited about it, but some of his stuff just wasn't my cup of tea."

"Yeah? What was your favorite?"

"A *Midsummer Night's Dream*."

"And what was your least favorite?"

"Um…probably *The Rape of Lucrece*."

"What on earth is that?"

"It's one of Shakespeare's sonnets. I have to say, his famous plays are great. His lesser-known works—not so much. But I can now offer that I've read all the works of Shakespeare as party conversation."

Tyler looked back down at the sheet of paper. "And you know how to speak French?"

"Oui, monsieur. Je parle Français très bien."

"You said you speak French very well, right?"

"That's right. Do you speak French, too?"

Tyler winced. "No, but I knew someone that spoke it frequently. Although, I'm convinced not fluently."

He lowered his head to study the page again, and Lilah put a hand on his arm. "Are you planning to quiz me?"

"Yup, because I've got to know about the hot-air balloon ride."

"Well, that was just a state fair event. They had this big open field, and you could pay to go up in the balloon for a few minutes. Now if I'd been in the wilds of Africa or over the Swiss Alps then maybe that would have been something. But, as it was, all I got was a really good view of more cornfields. Plus, I discovered right then and there that I'm afraid of heights. What about you? Are you afraid of heights?"

Tyler shook his head. "No, I don't think so. Reggie and I spent a lot of time climbing trees as kids." He looked back at The List. "You can play the guitar? I wish I had one so you could serenade me."

"It's just as well that you don't. I can't play very well."

"But you have it crossed off The List."

"That's because it's written as 'learn to play the guitar.' I had three guitar lessons and came to the realization that I would never be a skillful guitar player. But I did learn. And before you ask, the same rule applies to karate. I don't know karate, but I did take some lessons. So if we're mugged in an alley, you're on your own."

"I actually do know karate," Tyler said.

"Get out of here? Really?"

"Tae Kwon Do actually. But, yeah. I didn't get all the way up to black belt status, but it's safe to say that if we get mugged in an alley, I've got your back."

"See, now that's good to know."

Tyler shook his head. "I guess the previous rules apply to 'Learn to rap'?"

"That's right," Lilah joked. "It was a six-week course at Devry University, and I got my bachelor's degree in Rap."

"What?"

"I'm just kidding. It was a talent show in college. A bunch of us girls did a stupid rap about college life to the tune of LL Cool J's 'Around the Way Girl.'"

Tyler laughed. "This list is like a map of your life. I'm getting to know things about you that might not have ever come up in conversation."

"Yeah," Lilah answered, feeling nostalgic. "It's funny because you walk around in life feeling like you've never done anything, but when you write it all down and look at it this way, you realize you've done more than you think."

Tyler continued to scan The List. "I was around when some of these things got done. Let me see...*kiss a stranger* is me, right?"

"Yes, you weren't a complete stranger, but close enough."

"Good, when you look back over the experiences you've had in New York, you won't be able to think about them without thinking of me."

"That goes without saying. There's no way I would think of this trip without thinking of you."

Tyler put The List down and leaned toward her. "Okay, now there's one more thing on your list that I want to take part in."

"What's that?" Lilah asked, her thoughts still focused on the accomplishments of her trip.

"Item number 38."

Lilah felt her whole body grow warm. "Item number 38?"

"Yes," he said, tugging the T-shirt over her head. "I've been doing some research, and I think we can get that done. I'm willing to dedicate the rest of the day to accomplishing the task."

Chapter 18

Lilah didn't get back to her hotel until late Sunday evening. Tyler hadn't wanted to let her leave, but she couldn't go another day without fresh clothes. As soon as she let herself into the room, the phone was ringing. "Hello?"

"Wow, it must have been good. I've been calling since yesterday."

"Hi, Angie," Lilah said, feeling her cheeks warm with embarrassment.

"Sooo?"

Lilah sucked in a deep breath. It was hard to talk about her feelings for Tyler. That made them real. But Lilah knew it would be futile to try to put Angie off.

"I had a great time…visiting. Tyler is a wonderful…host."

"Okay, Queen of the Euphemism. I'm glad to hear that. Can I ask one more question before your head explodes into a million pieces from the embarrassment?"

"What is it?"

"What are you going to do about Reggie?"

"Reggie who?"

"Reggie Martin. Number one on your list. Are you still planning to have a date with him?"

Lilah could honestly say that after Saturday night, she hadn't given Reggie a second thought. "It's not as complicated as it sounds. To check the item off The List all I need is something that qualifies as a date. It could even be a double date where I'm with Tyler and Reggie brings someone else. You see? I wouldn't be going behind Tyler's back. It'll work out somehow," she said.

"I don't think I've ever heard you sound this worry-free."

"I'm living in the moment and it feels good."

"Good for you. But you sound tired. Didn't get much sleep, did you?"

Lilah giggled. "No, not much. But item 38? Check."

Lilah stared down at the plate in front of her. She smiled prettily at the waiter, but as soon as he walked away, she looked imploringly at Tyler.

"I didn't think they'd still be in the shell."

"They're snails. What were you expecting?"

"I wasn't expecting them to look like snails. I thought they'd be in a sauce over pasta or something. You know, like food."

Tyler gave her a sympathetic smile, then took a hearty bite of his shrimp cocktail. He'd brought her to one of the most romantic French restaurants in New York so she could try escargot. But now that she had it in front of her, she was having second thoughts.

She stared down at the fine bone-china plate, but she couldn't get past the tiny snail shells arranged in a neat little circle. Beside the plate was a strange pair of tongs, obviously meant to hold the shells stable while she picked out the meat with the tiny fork.

Taking a healthy gulp of wine, Lilah picked up the tongs. "Are you sure you don't want to get in on this?"

"Hell no," Tyler said without hesitation. "That's all you."

"Okay, here goes nothing." Lilah grasped the first tiny shell in her tongs, bringing it up to her face for closer inspection.

Holding the tongs in one hand, she approached the shell with her tiny fork. She must have been gripping the tongs too tightly because as she probed the shell with her fork, the snail shell sprang out of her grasp and across the table.

It landed with a plop in Tyler's shrimp cocktail.

Lilah covered her mouth. "Oops. I'm so sorry," and then she couldn't suppress a peal of laughter that escaped from her lips.

Tyler gave her a wry look as he picked up his spoon to fish the snail out of his cocktail glass. "Yeah, you look really sorry, too. I distinctly remember telling you that I didn't care for any."

He placed the snail neatly back on her plate, though now it was liberally coated with a tangy red sauce.

Lilah shrugged. "Who knows, maybe it's better that way."

Tyler shook his head in exasperation as Lilah giggled. "Quit stalling, Lilah. You can't have your filet mignon until you finish your escargot. Or better yet, just eat one."

Lilah bit her lip. "It's harder than it looks."

Then, to further Lilah's embarrassment, a passing waiter must have heard her last comment. "Madame, do you need some help?"

He then proceeded to instruct her on the proper way to grip the tongs and pry out the delicious morsel. With the snail now skewered by her tiny fork, Lilah no longer had any means of stalling.

She nodded politely at the waiter until he walked

away. She didn't know what was about to happen, but she was sure she didn't need an audience.

Lifting the fork to her mouth, she popped in the escargot and began chewing rapidly. The most dominant flavors were garlic and butter.

Tyler was watching her with unveiled disgust. "How is it? Is it nasty?"

Lilah shrugged. "You know, actually…it's not that bad. It's chewy." She pushed the plate away. "I could probably go on eating it, but I can't get my mind past what it is. So, eat escargot…check."

Tyler smiled. "Good job. Now let's find the waiter and have him take it away before I lose my appetite."

"You big baby. They weren't that bad."

He made another face. "They definitely don't look like they belong on a dinner table. They should be out on the street crawling free."

"Well, don't worry. I know what will take your mind off that."

Tyler sat a little straighter, picking up the seductive tone in her voice. "I'm listening."

It was a quiet, romantically lit restaurant, so Lilah didn't want to say the words out loud. *I'm not wearing any underwear,* she mouthed to him.

She watched a slow smile curve his lips as her message soaked in.

"Really…" All of his masculine appreciation

came through in just that one word. "Is that a treat for me?"

Lilah gave him a coy smile. "It's on The List."

She'd been hesitant at first. But now that she was sitting across from Tyler, she was glad she'd gone for it. Her simple black silk sheath fell below her knees, protecting her modesty, while silhouetting her curves to their best advantage.

"Have I mentioned," Tyler said softly, "how much I love your list? When you're through with this one, I have some suggestions for the next one."

"Like what?"

He winked at her. "I'll write them down for you."

A thrill rushed up Lilah's spine. Tyler's words implied that he planned to be around for a while. The thought of having him in her future felt really good.

He didn't know how he'd made it through dinner, Tyler thought as he rushed Lilah into his apartment. Ever since she'd mouthed the words to him, all he'd been able to think about was the fact that she wasn't wearing any underwear.

As soon as the apartment door closed behind them, he was pulling Lilah back into his arms. While his lips found hers in a hot, breathless kiss, his hands slid down her back. He joined the smooth glide of his palms from her waist to her hips then back up to cup her derriere.

Lilah's soft hands were stroking the muscles in his neck, which felt bunched and tight in his urgency. Gathering the fabric of her skirt, Tyler dipped his hands under the hem. And they met skin. Wonderful, soft smooth skin.

A wave of heat surged through him and he was lifting her. He raised her until her legs could circle his waist, then he turned until Lilah's back was against the wall.

His lips and teeth nipped and sucked at her neck, while he reveled in the feel of her bare skin beneath his hands. Lilah made soft gasping sounds as she fought the buttons on his shirt. She tugged and pulled until he could shrug off his coat and shirt in one motion.

Then her hands were everywhere. She played with the tiny points of his nipples and the long ridges of his back. Then her hands were dipping lower into the waistband of his slacks.

Even with the support of the wall, Tyler felt his knees growing weak. They weren't going to make it to the bedroom. With Lilah still wrapped around him, he took a step back. He lifted her until Lilah's feet could touch the floor, then he stripped her dress over her head in one motion.

Using their discarded clothing as a pallet, he laid her out on the carpet. The sight of Lilah's nude form outstretched and waiting for him sent Tyler over the edge. There wasn't time to pull off his pants. With his remaining energy, he freed himself to put on the condom he'd taken from his wallet.

Then he lowered himself over her. Using his fingers to make her ready for him, he surged into her body. And together they hurtled into a new realm of sensation.

Chapter 19

"You're not jealous, are you?" Lilah asked Angie as they strolled down Madison Avenue.

"Maybe a little bit. But I realize this isn't all about me."

"Don't say that. I wouldn't even be here without your encouragement."

"But I wouldn't dream of standing in your way. I would hate for you to miss out on the experience of a lifetime because you're worried about my feelings."

"I feel so foolish. You know this really isn't my style. And I'm still not convinced that I'm cut out for this."

"Nonsense. He's perfect for you. You'll see."

They stepped off the sidewalk into the Luigi Giuliano designer boutique. Today she and Angie were shopping for the designer dress she would wear on her thirtieth birthday. She was going to really have to ramp up her real estate sales when she got home to justify the lofty price tags they'd been reviewing all afternoon.

"I still think, if you design something and charge me a lot of money for it, that would count."

"For the last time, hush. Now, we've been to seven stores and you won't commit to anything. But I'm convinced Giuliano is perfect for you. Very tailored with a sexy edge. I think his styles will flatter your curves."

When Lilah had added *own an expensive designer dress* to her list, they had still been in college. Angie had recently become obsessed with fashion, and they'd spent hours poring over fashion magazines and dreaming of becoming rich and famous enough to own such things of their own.

Since those days, Lilah had worn business suits to the office and jeans around the house. For the last several years, she'd been so far removed from that life that she didn't know what was in style and what wasn't.

But Angie, on the other hand, was a force to be reckoned with. She knew all the designer names and had spent the morning explaining the tips and tricks to finding clothes that flattered her petite figure.

To Lilah's surprise, she finally found *the* dress in Luigi Giuliano's store. It was emerald-green and complemented her complexion perfectly. She'd known the second she saw the airy silk fabric that she had to have it.

The material was gathered over her breasts, which she'd always worried were on the small side until she saw them in this dress. The dress was sleeveless except for the bands of material that draped her arms just below her bared shoulders. The empire waist clung to her form until it flared gracefully around her hips. The short flirty hem ended mid-thigh, making her feel fresh and young.

The full-service boutique was going to make some custom alterations and send the dress to her hotel by Friday. Lilah clapped her hands with excitement as they left the store.

"Yea. I don't even think I was this excited about my wedding dress."

"Thanks a lot." Angie punched her in the arm because she'd been the one to make it.

"Sorry. You know what I mean. I've never had a dress like that before. I didn't even know I wanted one until now. For the first time, I think I'm actually looking forward to my birthday party."

"That's because you have a boyfriend."

"I don't have a boyfriend."

"Even if you're not ready to call him that, it's still true."

"No—"

"Do you have any idea how different you've been since you've been with Tyler?"

Lilah frowned. "Different? I'm sorry, I didn't mean to—"

"No, I mean in a good way. You're not making excuses anymore. Excuses not to enjoy yourself. Excuses not to live in the moment. You're back to your old self, the way you were before Chuck—"

"You've noticed that much of a change?"

"Hell yeah. But I think it was your marriage that changed you. Now that you've finally stopped punishing yourself enough to let someone else in, I think you're recovering your old spirit."

How had she become so disconnected with herself? This time in New York had refreshed her soul in a lot of ways. The List had forced her to stop listening to that fearful voice in her head that held her back.

Nothing on her list was practical, but the act of doing some of those things had been truly liberating. Allowing herself to love Tyler—

Love Tyler? Was she in love? Lilah was so startled by that thought she stopped in the middle of the sidewalk.

Angie turned around. "What's wrong? What happened?"

"Nothing, I guess I was just realizing that you're right. It feels good to get back to myself again. It's been a while since I've felt so free."

Angie slipped her arm through Lilah's and tugged her along. "Now that's what I like to hear. Now aren't you glad I talked you into coming to New York?"

"I'm very glad I came." Lilah had come to New York to complete The List with Angie. However for the last few days, she and Tyler had been working on it together. "Can I ask you a question?"

"What is it?"

"I came to New York to spend time with you. Are you upset that I've been spending so much time with Tyler?"

Angie rolled her eyes. "Girl, don't you know me better than that?"

"I just mean that there were a few things on The List we'd planned to do together that I ended up doing with Tyler."

"It's been great having you here, Lilah. But to be honest with you, some of the late nights were getting to me. Besides we both knew there were a couple of things on that list that I was not going to be able to help you with."

Lilah laughed with Angie. "Okay, good. And how is everything going at work?"

"Nothing worth mentioning." Angie's face

clouded for a moment, making Lilah wonder if her friend was holding something back.

"Don't worry, you're too talented to be a costume designer off-Broadway for much longer. Keep in mind that you can move back to D.C. and design clothes for me exclusively."

"Yeah, right. If I charged you for all the clothes that I'd made for you over the years, you'd know that you couldn't afford me."

Lilah laughed. "I know that's right."

Once back at her hotel, Lilah went straight to work, finishing the scarf she'd been knitting for Tyler. Thankfully, she was nearly done, but it had been difficult to work on it over the last several days with Tyler around so much. It wasn't the most beautiful scarf in the world, but she knew Tyler was the kind of man who would be able to appreciate the fact that she'd made it with love.

Oh God. There was that word again. She was in love with Tyler. After her divorce, Lilah didn't know that she was even capable of falling in love again. Now she realized that what she was feeling with Tyler in no way resembled what she'd shared with Chuck.

It wasn't that she hadn't loved her ex-husband, but it now felt a lot more like friendship than grand passion. She'd thought that kind of love was for novels. But Tyler never acted jealous of her time spent elsewhere. He was happy to be with her, but he had a life of his own and was a complete person without her.

Chuck's favorite phrase was that she completed him. It was too much pressure to be everything to someone. It was nice to know that Tyler wasn't insecure. Lilah found that incredibly sexy.

Now the big question was…did Tyler love her?

Lilah's List Blog Entry, November 7, 2007

I don't know if anyone's reading this blog besides my friends—shout out to Angie and Maureen— but, just in case someone else out there cares, I've been so scarce lately because it's easier to write when I'm upset or stressed out. Lately, I've been so happy, I haven't had the pathos needed to pour my heart out on the World Wide Web.

Tyler closed his browser. He couldn't read Lilah's blog anymore. He felt like he was invading her privacy. Fortunately she hadn't gotten specific in reference to him, but she'd made it clear that there was a man in her life and that she was happier than she'd been in a long time.

He went to the phone and dialed Reggie's cell. He got his voice mail again. For the last two days he hadn't heard a word from his brother, and Tyler knew exactly what the problem was.

They'd gotten Reggie's full support team together to discuss the national tour he'd been begging for. Reggie hadn't been pleased to hear that the group wasn't ready to back him on the scale he'd wanted.

Reggie was expecting a luxury tour bus, an A-list backup band and dates booked at super-dome arenas branching from the west to the east coast.

Tyler thought a tour was a great way for his brother to showcase his talent and get up close and personal with his core fan base. But, the fact was, Reggie couldn't afford to finance the grand tour he envisioned, and his record label wouldn't even consider it.

If Reggie wanted to tour, he was going to have to do small club venues, sticking to one of the coasts to cut travel costs.

Reggie's problem was that he wanted every-thing overnight. And nothing worth having could be achieved that way.

Tyler sighed, walking away from the phone. This was the worst possible time for Reggie to be pitching a fit. Tyler needed him and he needed him right now.

He had to set up a meeting with Lilah and Reggie. Tyler didn't want to be the reason Lilah couldn't complete her list. When he could have gotten Reggie to show up whenever he'd wanted, Tyler had kept him away. Now that he *wanted* Reggie to get together with Lilah, the kid was nowhere to be found.

With Reggie in this mood, there was no telling how a meeting with Lilah would go. If he did show up, he might sulk and barely speak to her, or Reggie might throw him under the bus by telling her that Tyler hadn't worked that hard to arrange a meeting.

Tyler paced the room. Lilah's birthday was Saturday, so he had to sort this out immediately. Picking up his keys, he headed out the door. There wasn't time to waste. He had to go find his brother right now.

Lilah came out of Tyler's kitchen and sat beside him on the sofa. "That talking stove is pretty tricky, but I think I've figured it out. The roast has about fifteen more minutes, then we can eat."

"Great."

"What's the matter, Tyler? You've been preoccupied all evening."

He squeezed her knee. "I'm sorry, Lilah. I didn't mean to neglect you. It's Reggie. He's giving me the cold shoulder. He's still not talking to me."

"He's still upset about the tour thing you told me about?"

"Yeah, can you believe when I went over to his apartment today, he wouldn't even open the door?"

"Wow, are you serious?" She began kneading the tension out of his shoulder muscles. "Don't let it get to you. I'm sure he'll calm down in a few days."

Tyler sighed heavily. "You don't have a few days. I don't know how I can arrange a meeting between the two of you if he won't even see me."

"Don't worry about that. My list isn't that important. To be honest with you, it's fairly ridiculous for me to think I need a date with a celebrity I barely know. These last two weeks have shown me that each individual item on The List isn't what matters. What matters is that I know when I put my mind to something, I can make it happen. After all the great adventures I've had, I couldn't care less whether I ever get a date with Reggie Martin. I'd much rather date you."

Tyler reached back and squeezed her hands. "I hear what you're saying, but that's not good enough for me. I'd hate to send you home to D.C. knowing that you didn't complete The List because of me."

"It wouldn't be your fault, Tyler."

"Actually, it would be. Lilah—"

She climbed onto his lap, forcing his back against the cushions. "You're stressing yourself out. I'm going to have to insist that you relax."

"But I wanted to—"

"Shh. We've only got fifteen minutes, so that doesn't leave any time for talking," she said, pulling her sweater over her head and pressing her lips to his.

Chapter 20

"What do you want for your birthday, Lilah?" Tyler asked as the two of them lay in bed that night.

"I don't know," Lilah said, propping herself up on one arm. "I honestly can't think of anything that I need."

"Birthday presents aren't about what you need. They're about what you want. Isn't there anything you want?"

Lilah thought about that for a few minutes. "Actually, Angie is throwing me a 'wild' party on Saturday. I think I'd like to have a special evening with just the two of us before then."

Tyler smiled. "I can do that. We'll do whatever you want. Do you have a restaurant you've been wanting to try?"

"I'm a huge fan of the Food Network show *Iron Chef America*, and I'd love to eat at Morimoto."

"Done. Anything else you'd like to do for your birthday?"

A wicked smiled came to her lips. "We can definitely revisit item number 38. But, before that, I'd love to go dancing. As much as we've been out on the town, there hasn't been any dancing."

"What kind of dancing do you mean? Ballroom or booty-shaking."

"Definitely booty-shaking. I'd like to learn ballroom dance, but I'll save that for the next list."

"Then it's a date. Since Reggie's still hung up on working with Jermaine Dupri in Atlanta, I'm trying to hook him up with a big-name producer locally. I've got a meeting with Pernell Weathers Friday evening, so can we do your birthday dinner tomorrow night?"

"That works for me. I can't wait."

"Are you sure you don't want to save this makeover for Saturday?" Angie asked Lilah while they sat side by side getting pedicures.

"No, I want to look great for Tyler tonight. I'm going to be leaving town on Sunday, and I want to make sure I leave an impression on him. We haven't talked about the future, but I want him thinking of me when I'm gone."

"With or without the makeover, I think he's pretty serious about you. Why don't you just tell him how you feel?"

"I'm not sure how I feel."

Angie snorted. "We didn't just meet yesterday. I know you. You're completely gaga over this guy. Why won't you just admit it?"

"Because I thought I was completely gaga over Chuck once, and we both know how that turned out."

"Nonsense. Tyler couldn't be more different from Chuck. Chuck sucked the life out of you. It's about time you were with a man who wasn't threatened by a confident woman."

Lilah sighed heavily. "I just can't think too far into the future. I'm just trying to concentrate on right now. And tonight I want Tyler to see the very best in me in every way. Did you finish the dress?"

"Of course. When we're done here, I'll go back to my apartment and get it while you check out of your hotel."

Angie had convinced Lilah to spend her birthday weekend in the penthouse suite at the Grande hotel, where her party would take place. While Lilah had been reluctant at first, she was now very excited about it.

These were the last days of her twenties. Why not live it up?

After the manicure, pedicure, massage and body polish, Lilah was getting her hair styled. She was apprehensive when Monroe, the stylist, suggested she try red highlights and a layered cut, but she decided to cross her fingers and go for it.

The result was better than she could have imagined. Monroe had added some warm red tones to her honey-colored hair, then had cut in some deep layers. When she shook her head, her curls bounced and swirled like the women in shampoo commercials.

Monroe whistled at her as he removed the drape. "Now, girl, that is a real New York hairstyle. You are ready to work it. I hope you have a banging outfit to wear to really set it off."

"I sure do. That's my designer over there," she said, pointing to Angie who was waiting in the lounge. "She made a fantastic dress just for me. Angela Snow. Watch out for her. She's going to be the next big name in fashion. You just wait."

"Well okay, girl. You go get 'em."

"I can't believe you're leaving us like this," Maureen wailed as Lilah stood before her with her luggage at her feet.

"I'm sorry. Believe me, I had a wonderful stay here at the Casablanca. I'll definitely come back."

"At least I'll see you at your birthday party Saturday night. I told my boyfriend and he can't believe we're going to be in the penthouse of the Grande hotel."

"I'm just glad you're going to be there. To be honest with you, I'm not even sure who, if anyone, is going to show up."

Maureen looked sly. "Oh, I think there will be a lot more than you think."

Lilah leaned forward to study the other woman. "Why? What do you know?"

She closed her lips and shook her head, as if to say she'd never tell. "You look fantastic, by the way. Didn't I tell you Monroe is a genius?"

"You've never steered me wrong, Maureen. I can't imagine what I would have done without you."

Maureen came around the desk to hug her goodbye, the bellman carried her bags out to the car where Sanjay was waiting.

Lilah didn't know why, but she felt like she was about to embark on yet another adventure within her adventure.

Standing in front of the mirror in her luxury suite, Lilah felt like a princess.

With all the beauty preparations she'd made today, she felt like she was getting ready for an important occasion. In her mind, she knew it was one.

Lilah didn't want to go back to D.C. without telling Tyler that she loved him. If she'd learned anything during this time in New York, it was that life was meant to be lived, not watched.

She wanted to create a romantic memory of the first time she said the words out loud to him. And she hoped her feelings would be returned.

Everything was working out perfectly so far.

She'd worried whether her new hairstyle would maintain its salon sheen into the evening, and it was still hanging in radiant waves to her shoulders.

"I knew it," Angie said, entering the room. "The dress is perfect on you."

"I know you're not going to believe me, but this dress is way better than the designer dress we bought. I love it so much, I may never take it off."

Angie had constructed a perfect optical illusion. The lilac fabric appeared to be transparent, but when Lilah moved it shimmered and sparkled in the light with tiny beads. The delicate beaded straps fastened behind her neck, narrowing into a sparkling broach, like a built-in necklace. The bodice branched into endless layers of diaphanous fabric.

It was elegant and feminine, like Lilah, with hints of Angie's edgy over-the-top flair. Lilah had picked up a matching clutch in the hotel gift shop that afternoon, and had carried it to the register without a glance at the price tag. Another list item complete.

"I'm ignoring the blasphemy that just came out

of your mouth, because I'm too busy admiring my own genius."

"I'm paying for this. And I won't take no for an answer."

Before Angie could rehash their argument, Lilah's cell phone started ringing.

"Hello?"

There was a pause on the line, leading Lilah to think she might have a prank caller.

"Hello?"

"Lilah, I have bad news," Tyler said.

Her heart immediately leaped into her throat. "What is it?"

"Pernell Weathers is getting on a plane for the West Coast tomorrow. I can't talk to him unless I catch up with him tonight."

Her heart sank and she immediately felt the sting of tears in her eyes. "It's okay. I understand."

"I'm so sorry, Lilah. Normally, I'd blow it off, but Reggie's still upset with me, and you still need to meet with him, so…"

"You don't have to explain. I really do understand." She'd been looking forward to this evening more than her actual birthday, but she didn't want Tyler to feel worse. His voice was already heavy with remorse.

"No, seriously, I feel terrible. I'll call you as soon as I get out of this meeting. Unfortunately, I don't know how long it will take."

"Stop worrying. It's fine. It's not as if you're missing my real birthday. As long as you're there on Saturday, that's all that matters."

"I'll make this up to you. I promise."

"I'll hold you to that."

Angie stood with her hands on her hips. "What happened?"

Lilah tucked her phone into her purse. "Do you want to have dinner at Morimoto with me tonight?"

"Just as soon as I can change."

Angie, not to be outdone by Lilah's blinging attire, returned from her apartment wearing a crimson catsuit with a plunging neckline and flared pant legs.

When the two women headed down to the lobby for their night out, Lilah was shocked to discover that Sanjay had arrived in a black stretch limousine.

"Ladies," he said, holding the door open for them.

Angie slid right in, but Lilah stopped and grabbed Sanjay's shoulder. "You've upgraded your ride. How did this happen?"

Sanjay dropped his professional facade and swung Lilah into a big hug. "This is all thanks to you, Lilah. Several customers read about me in your blog and have been asking my brother about my services. He was so impressed, he's agreed to let me drive his limousines on a trial basis."

Lilah gave him a high five. "Congratulations, Sanjay. I knew you could do it. But I don't understand how my blog could have helped you. There couldn't be enough people—"

"Didn't you see it?"

"Didn't we see what?" Angie asked.

"The Manhattan Underground." Sanjay dug under his front seat then passed a copy to them through the glass partition.

And there it was, a small blurb on the lower left corner of the page, touting Lilah's List as a quirky new must-read blog.

"I can't believe this. Is this a joke?"

Angie shook her head. "I think one of Tyler's friends from the karaoke bar mentioned *The Manhattan Underground.* She must have been the one to write you up. This calls for a toast," Angie said, reaching for the flutes in the minibar.

Angie and Lilah had a terrific time riding in the back of the limousine, blasting hip-hop music and drinking champagne. The only thing missing was Tyler. She couldn't wait to tell him all about it later that night.

After a spectacular dinner, Sanjay drove them to Monarch. The trendy new nightclub that Tyler had promised to take her to.

Lilah spotted the line winding around the block, and grabbed Angie's hand. "Uh, oh, déjà vu. Are we going to be able to get into this place without Tyler?"

"Girl, you've got to have confidence. We can do this," she said, pushing Lilah toward the door as Sanjay opened it for them.

Lilah stepped onto the pavement right in front of the velvet rope. Two hulking guys were working the door, and there were two lines. One was clearly for the regular folks because it was long and wound around the corner. The other seemed to be for VIPs, but even they were being kept waiting.

Lilah paused, rolling her eyes. "This is ridiculous."

Nevertheless, she took a deep breath and marched over to the two doormen standing between the two lines. The first guy, a tall gorgeous blond with a clipboard, barely glanced up.

"Is your name on the list?"

Lilah felt certain that it wasn't. Still she said, "Absolutely, Lilah Banks."

The guy started searching his list, but she saw the other doorman beside him looking her up and down. "Lilah Banks. Are you Remy's friend?"

Hope leaped in her heart. "Yes!"

The blonde's head popped up from his clipboard. "Lilah of Lilah's List? I've been reading your blog."

"You have?" Lilah asked incredulously.

He was already opening the rope for her.

"Come right in." As he ushered them through the ropes, she heard him speak into his walkie-talkie, "We have filet mignon coming through."

From his spot at the back of the VIP line, Reggie Martin stared in surprise. "Who was that?"

He'd been told no one but no one got into Monarch without waiting in line, celebrities and average Joes alike. But, suddenly, after a few words with the bouncers, this woman was being let through only seconds after stepping out of her limo.

Reggie shook his head. Either he was an even bigger loser than he'd thought, or that woman was someone very special.

Chapter 21

The two women entered the club and a hostess met them in the hallway to take their coats. Angie grabbed her arm and whispered in her ear, "Did you hear that? They called us filet mignon. I told you it was real."

"I'm going to have to thank Remy for putting in a good word for us."

"Good word, nothing. Didn't you hear him? He was reading your blog."

Lilah shook her head, still unable to comprehend the fact that word of her blog had spread so quickly. Her blog wasn't anything special. In fact, it was one of millions on the Internet.

With their coats checked in the front, Lilah and

Angie followed the woman into the swanky night-club. Lilah didn't want to look like a kid at an amusement park, but since visiting New York, she still hadn't adjusted to the amazing interior designs her eyes had been feasting on.

The room that spread out before them was made for elegant lounging. Plush chaises, plump, red, lip-shaped sofas, cubes and egglike capsules were arranged in clusters for perching and people-watching. Each cluster featured a brightly colored shaggy rug.

A ring of neon-lit steps led to the round sunken dance floor area. The wall behind the DJ booth was a running waterfall, lit with bright lights that faded from deep pink, blue and green.

But Angie and Lilah were led past all of this to a staircase beside the bar. At the top of the stairs, the woman introduced them to the two bouncers guarding the glass doors of the VIP lounge.

Once inside, Lilah discovered a room decked out for an emperor, with its own bar, dance floor and DJ. Around the dance floor were gilt lounge chairs and ornately carved love seats. They were led past a Grecian-style fountain with nymphs pouring water from their marble pots.

The woman they had been following led them to their area and took their drink orders. Exchanging looks, Lilah arranged herself on the recliner and Angie took the love seat. Seconds later, a bare-chested man wearing a toga and sandals, brought them a bowl of fresh fruit and goblets of water along with their drinks from the bar. It would have been perfect if Tyler had been there.

Once they were alone, Angie picked up her cosmopolitan and took a sip. "Now this is the life-style to which I intend to become accustomed."

Lilah sat forward, too anxious to eat or drink anything. "I don't know who they think we are, but I hope they don't figure out that we're frauds."

Angie shook her head. "Stop that. It's not your connection to Remy, and it's not a mistake. It's you and your blog."

Lilah shook her head in disbelief, hearing the pulsing beat of music for the first time. Even though she'd planned to share this experience with Tyler, there was no reason not to have fun. "Come on, let's dance."

After ten minutes of waiting out in the cold, Reggie and his friends were finally let into Monarch. As he and his crew were led to the VIP lounge, he couldn't help stewing over the fact that his clout still wasn't what he wanted it to be.

There she is!

Reggie's eyes immediately went to the middle of the dance floor where the woman he'd seen earlier and her friend were dancing.

She moved like she owned the world, taking

center stage while everyone else seemed to revolve around her.

Who was she?

He turned to his friend. "Jay, do you know who that girl is?"

His friend squinted at the dance floor. "Who?"

"That girl in the purple. She looks familiar, but I can't place her."

Jay shrugged. "I don't know her. She's hot, though. Want me to bring her over?"

Reggie shook his head. "Not yet."

She didn't look like the groupie type who would jump at the chance to meet him. Shoot, the way his luck was going, she probably didn't even know who he was.

Angie leaned down to speak into Lilah's ear. "Don't look now, but I think Reggie Martin just came in."

Lilah froze. "Where?"

"Hey, I said don't look. He's to your left. Looks like his table is directly opposite ours across the dance floor."

Lilah tried to sneak a peek, while she pretended to keep dancing. "What should I do?"

"Isn't it obvious? Go over to him."

Lilah's heart was pounding in her chest. He was here. The man she'd been working overtime to get to since she'd arrived in New York City.

But for some reason, Lilah couldn't get her feet to move. Lately she'd gotten it into her head that Tyler would be there when she and Reggie saw each other again. Without him around, it seemed really strange to approach his brother. He might get the wrong idea.

Then she'd have to explain that she'd been seeing Tyler and—

Lilah shook her head and walked off the dance floor. It was too confusing. She needed to talk to Tyler right away.

Lilah walked over to her sitting area and picked up her cell phone, but she didn't have enough signal. She'd have to try again from a better location.

Angie sat next to her. "What's going on?"

"I was trying to call Tyler, but I don't have any signal."

Her friend shrugged. "Okay, so you'll catch him up later. Bear in mind that you're about to miss a rare opportunity. Your birthday is in two days. You need to get this over with. Just go over there and offer to buy him a drink. Trust me. He'll go for it."

"No. I don't have to."

"What? Why not?"

"Because he's already headed this way."

The more Reggie looked over at the mystery woman, the more he was certain he knew her from somewhere. Was it another event or party? He wasn't sure, but it was driving him crazy.

Finally he decided the only way to put himself out of his misery was to just go over and speak with her. He didn't know why he felt strangely nervous. He could just feel that she was someone important.

It had nothing to do with the way she'd just strolled in here as though she owned the place. It was the way she moved, the way she wore that dress like it was made for her, the way she commanded the space around her.

As he reached them, both women stood. "Hi, I'm Reggie Martin. I saw the two of you sitting over here alone, and I wanted to introduce myself. Women as lovely as you should never be left alone."

"Isn't he a charmer," the tall one said, with a hint of sarcasm.

But his mystery lady gave him a wide warm smile as she extended her hand. "Oh, we know who you are. No introduction necessary."

He shook her hand with both of his. "Since you know who I am, can I assume you're a fan?"

"Absolutely." She looked him in the eye, searching for something. "This is my best friend, Angie Snow, and I guess you don't recognize me. I'm Lilah. Lilah Banks?"

Reggie swallowed hard. He had met her before, and she expected him to know who she was. He had to play along until he figured it out. "Of course. You look gorgeous tonight."

Lilah smiled up at him. "This is so crazy. We've been trying to catch up for over a week, and then we just happen to run into each other here."

Now Reggie was beginning to sweat because he didn't have any idea what she was talking about. Maybe she had the wrong guy.

He put his hand on her shoulder and leaned down to her ear. "I'm sorry, I have to confess. I don't know what you're talking about. When were we supposed to meet?"

Lilah's brow furrowed in confusion. "Several different times over the last week. Didn't Tyler tell you about me? I was your tutor in high school math, remember? Lilah Banks."

Reggie drew in his breath in shock. The image of a quiet studious girl flashed in his mind. "Oh my God, Lilah!"

"Yes," she laughed. "You remember me now?"

"Of course. I'm sorry about earlier. I meet so many people, and I didn't want to hurt your feelings. But, in my defense, you've really grown up. You look fantastic."

"Thank you." A charming blush tinged her cheeks. "But seriously, hasn't Tyler mentioned me? The List?"

Reggie shook his head absently, still focused on the fact that this woman standing before him was the same mousy young girl who'd tutored him. "List?"

By the look on her face, Reggie began to realize this was more than just a misunderstanding.

"Why don't you refresh my memory?"

"Saturday is my thirtieth birthday. I came to New York to complete a list of fifty things I wanted to do before I turned thirty. I started it in high school." She blushed profusely before she continued. "The first item on The List was 'Date Reggie Martin.'"

Reggie couldn't help grinning. "That can certainly be arranged."

Lilah shook her head. "I thought that it was. Tyler said that he told you all about me, and that he would arrange a meeting with you. You don't know anything about this?"

Reggie snapped his finger. "Oh yeah, there was something about a dinner Saturday before last. An old friend. That was you? Yeah, Tyler was pissed that I missed that. If I'd realized, believe me, I would have been there." He turned on his most charming smile, expecting her to be placated.

Instead she seemed more upset. "Is that it? Just Saturday before last? What about last week?"

Reggie shrugged. "I was around last week."

Lilah was clearly angry at this point, and Reggie knew that he'd made a mistake. He just wasn't sure what it was. "Are you all right?"

"Sure. I'm fine." She shook her head, muttering, "When am I going to learn," under her breath.

Something had gone terribly wrong. There was more to this situation than he was seeing. Then the pieces began to come together. Last week, his brother didn't ask him to meet an old friend. He'd asked him to meet his new girlfriend.

Lilah.

His brother had finally wanted something bad enough not to share. He obviously hadn't wanted Reggie as competition.

But it was too late now. Lilah was angry with Tyler and Reggie was in the perfect position to use that to his advantage.

In the taxicab ride back to Reggie's apartment, Lilah couldn't stop fuming. All this time she'd thought Tyler was helping her, he'd really been lying to her.

What had he been thinking? That she'd be flattered when she found out? It wasn't flattering that he hadn't trusted her enough to know the difference between a high school crush and a shot at true love.

Love.

Ha. What did she know about it anyway? Lilah had thought she'd been in love with Chuck and look how that had turned out. Now once again she'd fallen for someone who didn't think she could function on her own.

Lord save her from manipulative men. She was giving up. No more men. Not for a very long time.

"Are you okay? You look tense," Reggie said.

"I'm fine. I think I might be getting a headache." What was she doing heading to the apartment of another man? She was taking care of her list, she told herself. This would qualify as a date, and it would probably also make Tyler very angry, she thought smugly.

She wouldn't have to tell him that nothing happened. She could let him draw his own conclusions when he found out that she and Reggie had finally gotten together.

Reggie paid the taxi driver and guided her into his apartment building. They were quiet as they rode the elevator up to his place.

Lilah's palms began to get clammy as he worked the lock. She shouldn't be here. What if Reggie didn't understand that she had no intentions of sleeping with him.

She'd made a mistake, she thought in a panic.

Just as Lilah was about to ask him to call her a cab home, he nudged her into the room and ducked out, closing the door behind him.

"What the—" She stared at the closed door in shock.

Lilah felt strange—like she was in a horror movie, and she'd just been locked in a room with a ferocious beast.

"Lilah."

Her head snapped around to see Tyler waiting for her.

Chapter 22

Lilah turned around in a complete circle trying to process the circumstances. Reggie was gone. Tyler was here.

"What are *you* doing here?"

He stood and started toward her. "I need to talk to you. Reggie called. He said you seemed pretty upset with me."

She crossed her arms over her chest. "You think? Tonight I discovered that this entire time that I've been in the city, you've been pretending to help me, when actually you've been working against me."

"Look, I know it seems that way on the surface, but that's not really the case at all."

Lilah's entire body felt cold. Numb. Her emotions had completely shut off. She didn't know who this man before her was at all. "I'm listening."

"My brother really is pretty flaky. I asked him to meet us at Sapa for dinner and he blew us off. He resents how much he has to rely on me, so he can be passive aggressive at times."

"And just what does that have to do with me?"

"When I got into the studio with him, I found out that he didn't show up on purpose. We'd already established that there was an attraction between us. I started to think he'd never be able to appreciate a woman like you."

Lilah's anger sparked up again. "So what if he can't? You knew from the start the 'date' had more to do with completing The List than any hopes for a real relationship."

"No, I didn't know that, Lilah. You forget that I was there when you were in high school and you had a huge crush on him. You, like so many women, were under his spell. Completely blind to his faults," Tyler said.

"So what…you felt that you needed to protect me from him. You think I don't have sense enough to make my own judgment calls? Did you honestly think that I hadn't learned a thing or two between sixteen and twenty-nine?"

"To be honest with you, Lilah, it had more to

do with what I wanted. I realized that I wanted you. And I didn't want anything to stand between us."

"You do realize that you sound like a stalker, don't you?"

"I know my behavior was illogical, maybe even irrational. But that's how love can be. It makes you do things and feel things that don't make sense."

Lilah shook her head. A wave of déjà vu washed over her. "You sound just like my ex-husband. He used to think that love was a good excuse for being needy and controlling. He was constantly jealous of any time I spent away from him. It didn't matter if it was a coworker, my family or even my best friend. He thought all my time should be for him alone. I can't believe I almost made the same mistake again."

"Lilah, you know our relationship isn't a mistake. This is just an argument. It's not something that has to end things between us."

"Oh things are definitely over between us. They were over the second you started lying to me."

"I may have misled you, but I don't think I ever lied."

"Really? What about that night at the country-western bar? I asked you point-blank if you had told your brother about me. You swore to me that I was mistaken. This wasn't a situation that got out of hand. You set out to manipulate me so you could have what you wanted. Never mind that it might not be what I wanted."

Tyler's eyes went cold and hard in a way she'd never seen them. "Oh, it's clear what you wanted. Reggie asks you to come home with him and you follow behind him without any hesitation. You think just because you're hiding under the disguise of a schoolmate that it makes you anything other than what you really are…a groupie."

"You have your nerve. I came here because I was angry, and I wasn't thinking about anything other than how upset you'd be when you found out I'd been here. I never had any intentions of doing anything with Reggie." She paused. "Why am I explaining myself to you?"

She spun around and headed for the door.

"Lilah, wait!"

She ignored him, closing the door behind him.

Tyler sank to the sofa, head in his hands. He'd been afraid of this. Now what was he going to do? Lilah was only in town for a couple more days, he didn't have a lot of time to patch things up.

She thought he was like her ex-husband. It was possible she wouldn't ever forgive him.

The door opened and his head snapped up. "Lilah?"

"Sorry, bro, it's just me. I saw Lilah come through the lobby. She had the doorman call her a cab. I take it from the look on your face that things didn't go well."

"They couldn't have gone worse."

Reggie sat beside him. "I'm sorry, man."

"Can I ask you a question?"

"Shoot."

"Why did you call me? You've barely spoken to me over the last week. This was your perfect opportunity to screw me over."

Reggie squinted at him. "Why would I do that to you? I know I can be self-centered sometimes, but at the end of the day, I know you've always got my back. It took me a few minutes to fill in the gaps. If I'd pieced things together sooner, I would have been able to cover for you. As it was, all I could do was give you the chance to talk her down off the ledge."

"Well, she jumped anyway. But thanks, kid. It's nice to know I haven't completely screwed up every relationship in my life."

"No, I don't have a right to be mad at you. I was actually kind of impressed that you finally decided to keep something for yourself. It wasn't until tonight that I realized how much you've been sacrificing for me."

Tyler waved it off, as he always did.

"No, seriously, man. I think it might be good for both of us if I go down to Atlanta for a while."

"You're still considering that? But Pernell Weathers—"

"It's never left my mind. I need this. And I think you need it, too. You need time to figure what you would be doing if you hadn't taken responsibility for my career. I need to be responsible for that from now on. All this glitz and glamour isn't you."

"Yeah, but it's all I know anymore."

"Now you'll have plenty of time to figure it out. We can talk in the morning. Do you want to stay here tonight?"

Tyler's first instinct was to say no, claim he was fine, and head back to his apartment. But the thought of the emptiness that waited for him there gave him pause. "Yeah, Reg. I think I would like to stay."

Reggie clapped him on the back. "Then the couch is all yours."

When Lilah got back to her hotel room, the first thing she did was call Angie. Now that the red haze that hung over her eyes had cleared, she realized she'd broken the girlfriend code. Never leave your friends to go home with a man.

After watching multiple mishaps between other girls in college the two of them had devised some rules between them. Never leave a friend who'd had too much to drink unattended. Never date your friend's ex. And most important, always leave with the girlfriend you came with—no matter how cute a guy might be.

Even if he's Reggie Martin.

"Hello?" Angie's groggy voice said into the phone.

"It's me. Were you sleeping?"

"Not anymore, what happened?"

"I'm sorry to wake you. I just wanted to apologize for leaving you tonight. I don't know what I was thinking."

"I know what you were thinking, you wanted to get back at Tyler."

"The List—"

"Trust me, I saw the look in your eyes, and The List was the last thing on your mind."

"Are you mad at me? Of course, you have a right to be."

"No, I'm not mad. Of course, I thought I was going to be sleeping on satin sheets tonight in your penthouse suite, but other than that, due to extenuating circumstances, you're pardoned for violating the girlfriend code."

"Thanks." Lilah sank down onto the satin sheets and let the tension out of her body like air escaping a balloon.

"You sound really sad. What happened after you left?"

"Reggie and I barely spoke on the cab ride back to his place, and I immediately started coming to my senses. You're right, The List was an afterthought. Mainly, I just wanted it to get back to Tyler that I found his brother without his help."

"Oh my God, you didn't do anything crazy, did you?"

"I was angry—I wasn't out of my head. Once we got outside his apartment, I was about to tell him I wanted to go home, but instead he unlocked the door and shoved me inside."

"Oh no," Angie shrieked.

"Relax, he didn't come in after me because Tyler was there waiting for us. He must have called him. Clearly he figured out that I was mad because Tyler and I had been together."

"Score points for Reggie. He did the decent thing. I didn't want to upset you, but I thought he was a real pig for rushing you out of there so fast. So, you and Tyler?"

"We talked. Or rather, we argued. I can't even remember everything that was said. Just that it's over."

"Don't you think it's romantic that he wanted you all to himself?"

"No, I don't think it's romantic. I think it's psychotic." Lilah realized too late that her voice was rising.

"Okay, sorry. I didn't mean to stir you back up. I just think the two of you could work through this."

"No, he's just like Chuck—controlling, manipulative, too insecure to allow me room to breathe."

"I don't think—never mind, this is still too fresh for you. Maybe tomorrow things will look different."

"Yeah," Lilah said curtly. She didn't want to talk any more and the last person she wanted to think about was Tyler.

After she hung up the phone, she got ready for bed quickly and pulled the covers over her head like she'd done as a little girl. As a child she'd been afraid of monsters in her closet, tonight, she was afraid of memories.

The next morning the world didn't look different, but the room sure did. It took her a moment to adjust to the fact that she wasn't back at her cute little boutique hotel Casablanca.

The bed was huge and the suite seemed cavernous with no one else around. Then all the memories of the night before trickled back into her thoughts and a heavy sadness overtook her.

Right now, all she wanted was to be home. Home was her Georgetown condo with its cobblestone stairs and the ice-blue shutters she loved so much. She wanted to be able to bury herself in work today, the way she'd done after her divorce.

She was divorced. She tested the words as she did sometimes, searching for the stabbing pain that accompanied the thought. Nothing. The good news was that, after a year and a half, she'd finally gotten over it.

And the bad news was that she was able to get over it because she found a new pain that cut much deeper. Tyler. Thinking of him brought back the physical pain in her chest that came with heartache. Was it because she loved him? Or was it just a case of the "fool me twice, shame on me" scenario?

After Chuck, she'd thought her relationship with Tyler was completely opposite the one she'd had with her husband. Now, she was discovering that she was still making the same mistakes. Lilah still could not trust herself to know what was good for her.

Overwhelmed with emotions, Lilah climbed out of bed. She needed to get out. Normally, when she felt the well spilling over, she emptied it by writing on her blog. But she couldn't do that right now.

What would she write? That meeting Reggie Martin again was one of the worst experiences of her life? There was no way to make sense of her feelings to another living person.

She just needed out. She needed to feel the sting of cold air on her face. She needed to see people milling in the streets. Lilah needed to see that life was going on even though her heart was breaking.

Chapter 23

Tyler awoke, fully dressed, on Reggie's couch. His neck and back ached, but those pains were nothing compared to the emptiness in his chest. He had to talk to Lilah.

"Good, you're finally up," Reggie called as he exited the kitchen.

"Yeah," Tyler muttered as he stretched and cracked his bones. "Thanks for letting me stay—"

"Can we talk now?"

Tyler was tempted to put him off. All he could think about was getting back to his apartment for a hot shower and then patching things up with Lilah.

But he could hear a sense of urgency in his brother's voice that was uncharacteristic of his mellow, carefree style.

"Sure, what's on your mind? Atlanta?"

"Yeah…Tyler, I'm going. I've made all the arrangements. I'm going to stay with my buddy down there. He's got his own studio in his basement. And Jermaine Dupri has agreed to put his spin on any new stuff we write."

Tyler ran his hands over his head. He felt like he'd just been ambushed. His mouth felt chalky and his eyes were doing their best to convince him to shut them for a few more hours. "And you want to go out there to write music?"

"Yes, like I was trying to explain last night, this will be good for both of us. It's more clear to me now how much of your life you've devoted to looking out for me. I've become dependant on that, even as I've resented it. You need to do whatever it is you would be doing if you weren't managing my career, and I need to sink or swim on my own. It's time."

Tyler stared at his brother. There was no easy grin curving his lips. Reggie was looking back at him, straight in the eyes like the man he'd become while Tyler wasn't looking.

"You know, kid—I'm sorry. *Reggie,* as much as I may not like to admit it, you're probably right. You need to figure things out on your own." His mind started working, and a list of details formed in his head. "Just make sure when you get out to Atlanta you set up a support team. You're going to need—"

Reggie held up his hand. "I've got it covered, bro. I've been watching you for years. Don't you think I've learned something by now?"

Tyler nodded. "So when are you leaving?"

"Next week. That gives me enough time to settle everything here. A friend is going to stay in the apartment while I'm gone."

Tyler opened his mouth to caution Reggie about who he let watch his place, then closed his mouth.

"Don't worry, Tyler. I'm still going to call you for advice when I need it. But for the immediate future...you're fired."

Tyler swore quietly under his breath. That last statement really put it in perspective. He needed to find something else to do with his life. Fortunately he had a few ideas.

Lilah let herself wander the streets outside her hotel, not really worrying about getting lost. She knew if she got too far afield she could call Sanjay and have him pick her up.

She tried to distract herself from her thoughts by letting herself get absorbed in the sights and sounds around her. New York was a busy place and it was filled with people rushing to their next destination.

Lilah had been in such a rush leading up to her thirtieth birthday, and now that it was a day away, she wasn't sure what all the fuss was about. It was just a number. One more year, on top of the last one.

As Lilah turned a corner, she found herself facing a crowd of people. They were all watching a podium in a town square where a man was speaking. There were several others milling about with signs.

Lilah moved closer, trying to figure out the cause of all the commotion. She listened as the man on the podium encouraged individuals to take ownership for one fraction of the homeless problem by offering time, effort and money. Then she followed the protestors as they marched down Madison Avenue with their signs protesting excess and waste while men, women and children went hungry.

By the time Lilah returned to her extravagant hotel suite that afternoon, she felt both invigorated and guilty at the same time.

Wasn't she guilty of the same thing? Her first fancy designer gown had been delivered that morning and she was preparing for an outlandish party. And at that very moment, she didn't want any of it.

Picking up the phone, she dialed Angie. "I

know you're not going to want to hear this, but I want to call off the party. I'm going to head back to D.C. tonight."

Lilah could only assume the lingering silence on the other end was because Angie had passed out from shock.

"I'm waiting for the punch line," she finally said. "This is a very bad joke, isn't it?"

"No, it's not. My heart just isn't in this anymore."

"But what about the rest of The List. What about your guests? There isn't time to contact everyone to call it off."

"I don't care about The List anymore. It's served its purpose. It taught me how to go after things that I want. I don't need it now. And as for the party—have it without me if you can't call it off. I'll pay for everything. I just want to go home."

"You can't go home. This is nonsense. Is this how you handle a spat with your lover? Just make up with him already and then we can party as scheduled."

"It's not that simple."

"Only because you refuse to let it be that simple. If you go home today, you've wasted all your time here."

"It wasn't a waste. I learned a lot about myself. For one thing, I'm still making the same mistakes, trusting the wrong people."

Angie sighed heavily into the phone. "Okay,

well, I didn't want to lay this on you. But you can't go home because I need you."

Lilah paused. Was something really wrong with her friend or was she saying the only thing she could to get her to stay? "You know if you really need me, I'm here for you. What's going on?"

"I lost my job."

"What? When did this happen?"

"Wednesday. Remember the diva with the platinum buttons that I replaced with silver?"

"Yes? Well, she broke out in a rash and insisted I be fired. In my defense, it was supposed to be hypoallergenic silver."

"Oh my God, Angie. Why didn't you tell me? Have I been that self-absorbed?"

"No, I've been in denial. It's been fun hanging out with you and planning this party. I thought I could go deal with my situation after you left town. If you leave today, I'm going to have to wallow in self-pity."

"I can't believe you kept this from me. There's no way I'm leaving now. You have to get over here. We can update your résumé and start looking through the paper for—"

"This is exactly what I didn't want to happen. Now you're going to focus on propping me up. I'll work on my résumé later. Right now, all I really want is for us to have fun together."

"We will have fun. I'll forget about my man

troubles, you'll forget about your job troubles and we'll live it up for the next twenty-four hours."

Tyler hung up the phone in frustration again. He should have expected this. Lilah wasn't taking his calls. The hotel must have been instructed not to put him through, because they were claiming she had checked out. And when he called her cell phone, it went straight to voice mail.

He knew she was upset, but what happened to second chances? What they'd started could really be something real. It was too important to throw away over one fight. He wasn't trying to downplay his mistakes, but Lilah was overreacting.

On the other hand, she was divorced, and she seemed to be drawing some heavy parallels between him and her ex-husband. He couldn't expect her forgiveness when she was still healing from the wounds of another relationship. All he'd done was come along and reopen them.

How could he make things right when she wouldn't even speak with him? Grabbing his coat, Tyler headed out the door. He needed to try to speak with her in person. Once she realized he wasn't going to let her run away from this, maybe he could win her back.

Stepping into the lobby of the Casablanca hotel, Tyler was tempted to just bypass the front desk and head up to Lilah's room. He knew the number, even though he'd never stayed over. But the guy on the phone had said she'd checked out. There was a small chance that she had been upset enough to head back to D.C.

He walked over to the front desk, praying that wasn't the case. "Excuse me," he said to the pretty redhead standing there. "I was wondering if you could help me. I'm looking for Lilah Banks. My name is Tyler Martin and—"

"Oh wow, any relation to Reggie Martin?"

Whenever possible, Tyler denied it, but today he could see it getting him somewhere. "Yes, he's my brother."

"Oh yes, I've seen you here before with Lilah. She must not have had a chance to tell you, she moved to the Grande hotel a couple of days early. We were sorry to see her go, but I'll be at her party Saturday."

"The Grande? Thank you so much."

"Hey, do you mind if I ask you if she ever got that date with your brother?"

"Uh—"

"You know what? Don't tell me. I'll ask her tomorrow. It's the big day, you know. She has to have everything done by then. I guess she's so busy running around she hasn't had time to update her blog. You'll be there, right?"

"I wouldn't miss it for the world. I guess I'll see you there."

"That's right. When you see her, tell her Maureen at the Casablanca is expecting juicy inside details, okay?"

"I'll tell her."

Chapter 24

Arriving at the Grande hotel, Tyler tried to plot his course of action. Since he didn't know Lilah's room number, he had to hope the front desk clerk here would be as helpful as the one at the Casablanca.

"Can I help you, sir?"

"Yes, I'm looking for one of your guests. Lilah Banks? Can you tell me which room she's in?"

"We can't give out room numbers, sir. But I'll call her and let her know you're here."

The desk clerk dialed and exchanged a few brief words, then handed him the phone.

Tyler's heart leaped. She was going to talk to him. "Hello?"

"I'm sorry, Tyler." It was Angie.

Tyler's heart sank. "Listen, Angie, is Lilah there? I really want to try to work things out with her."

"She's here, but she's not ready to talk."

"Really? Isn't there anything you can do? How can I fix this if she won't hear me out?"

"I know. I'm on your side, but I'm duty bound as her best friend to respect her wishes. I'll keep talking her through it, but after her divorce, she doesn't want to take a lot of risks. You hurt her once, she doesn't want to give you the chance to do it again."

"Can you at least tell me what room you're in?"

"I wish I could, but she'd kill me, and I can't help your cause if she won't speak to me, either."

After his disheartening talk with Angie, Tyler found himself at his brother's apartment.

"Hey," Reggie said when he opened the door. "Judging by the look on your face, things didn't go well with Lilah?"

Tyler walked in and slumped onto the couch. "I couldn't even talk to her. I went to the hotel where I thought she was staying, but the girl told me she'd moved to the Grande. I couldn't get past the lobby there. I don't get why she won't even talk it out with me."

"Didn't you two try that last night?"

"We argued mostly, but we can't leave things like that. I was hoping she would have cooled off after some time to think."

"Maybe you can speak to her at her party."

"It's in her suite, and I don't know which one it is. No, that's it. She's leaving New York after this weekend and I may never see her again. I've just got to accept that."

"So you're giving up?"

"What choice do I have? She won't take my calls. I can't see her. There's nothing more I can do."

"You can hang out in the lobby and wait for her to leave."

"No. That's crazy. Maybe she'll get back home, change her mind and call me. But until then, I just have to wait."

Reggie sank down on the sofa beside him and the two of them sat in silence.

Lilah woke up on her birthday and poked Angie in the ribs.

"What? I'm awake!"

"I don't feel any different."

"What do you mean?"

"It's my thirtieth birthday. I don't feel any different."

"How did you expect to feel?"

"Different. We've been making such a big deal about turning thirty that I expected to be struck by lightning and imparted with new wisdom."

"I could have told you that wasn't going to

happen. All you had to do was ask. I've been thirty for six months and here I am unemployed. No, there's no extra wisdom. Just extra pounds. After thirty I started gaining weight just for breathing."

"Oh yeah," Lilah said blandly. "You're a cow."

"I know I look thin, but I actually have to work at it now. The days of eating whatever I want without looking back are over. Don't say I didn't warn you."

"Well, I guess it's official. I failed The List."

"No, you still have today. You don't officially turn thirty until 11:29 p.m."

"What's the difference?"

"The difference is about fourteen hours. You shouldn't throw away all your progress because of a date on the calendar. Finish The List."

"To be honest, I couldn't care less about that list. It brought me many interesting adventures, but I definitely was wrong to make myself a slave to it. I think the real spirit of The List was to find experiences that I wanted to have and make them a priority."

"All I know is, tonight this suite will be filled with your friends, and you really should start getting ready. I have some details to attend to, and I'm going to need you out of my hair for a few hours."

"No, you did not just kick me out of my own room for the day."

"Yes, I did. But it's for a good cause. Now go get dressed."

Lilah was just coming out of the shower when she heard a knock on the door. It opened and she heard Angie speaking with someone.

The French doors leading to the bedroom were closed, so Lilah continued to dress. Angie was probably coordinating with someone from the hotel about the party.

She never heard anyone leave, so when Lilah was ready, she braced herself as she walked out into the outer room. Angie knew better than to let Tyler ambush her, didn't she?

"Hey, Lilah."

"What are you doing here?" she asked, then turned to stare at Angie as if to say, *Why did you let him in?*

Reggie stepped forward. "I thought we could have our date. That way you can cross it off your list once and for all."

Once again, Lilah looked back and forth between her friend and Reggie. "I don't understand."

"Sure you do." He took her hand and led her to the door. Angie grabbed Lilah's coat and purse, thrusting them into her hands.

"Don't come back before one," she said, pushing her out the door.

"Happy birthday, by the way," he said, stepping into the elevator with her. "I spent my thirtieth birthday in bed."

Lilah rolled her eyes, envisioning a harem of

scantily clad women. "I don't want to hear about it," she said, waving him off.

"No, not like you're thinking. I had a stomach virus. It had been going around, and I was too sick to go to the party Tyler planned for me. He canceled it to look after me. The next day, Tyler came down with it. I felt better so I went out to a strip club with my boys."

"Oh, I get it," Lilah said as they reached the lobby. "You've come here to talk up your brother. If that's the plan, spare me. It is my birthday, after all, consider it your gift to me."

"Actually, that little story pretty much summarizes my relationship with my brother. He looks out for me, and I do whatever I want. I'm not proud of it, but it was just what both of us were used to."

They headed out into the street, and Lilah realized that Reggie had an agenda and she wasn't going to be able to sway him from it. She decided she would quietly listen, and when he was done, she'd tell him to mind his own business. He had no idea what she'd been through.

"So, when Tyler came to me for advice on how to get your attention, I was surprised. He'd never asked my opinion on anything."

Lilah stopped in the middle of the sidewalk. "Wait a minute. I thought he hadn't told you about me."

"He didn't mention you by name. He told me

he'd met someone, and he wasn't sure how to approach you. I still didn't think much of it. But, looking back, that was a big turning point in our relationship. He finally saw me as an authority on something. My big brother needed me. It was pretty cool."

Lilah continued walking in silence. This was pointless. How did she get trapped in this conversation?

"But I knew things had changed the most when I found out that my brother had finally found something that was important enough to him not to share it."

"I hope you're not talking about me."

"Of course, I'm talking about you. Do you realize my brother gave me first pick of everything our whole lives? I didn't realize it myself until recently, but ever since we were kids, Tyler has felt the need to protect me. To make sure I always had everything I needed. I always thought he was on a power trip, trying to control me, parent me. But I was wrong."

They'd reached a small café and Reggie guided her in. Lilah stopped at the entrance. "Did you bring me here on purpose?"

"Yeah, this place makes the best sandwiches. Were you expecting something fancier? I guess we could go to—"

"No, I mean…Tyler brought me here. Is that why you picked this place?"

"I didn't know he'd brought you here before. I swear. Tyler used to work at a law firm around the corner, and he'd always have me meet him here for lunch. I used to get annoyed because he never wanted to eat anywhere else, but he said it was his favorite. I picked it out of habit. Would you rather go somewhere else?"

"No, I just—never mind. It's fine."

There was one empty table left by a large picture window. They placed their orders and then they fell into an awkward silence.

"Look, I can tell by your expression that you don't want to hear this. But you've got my brother painted in your mind as some kind of villain. You think what he did was selfish, and you're probably right. But that behavior was against his nature. You were the first person my brother has ever placed ahead of me. To you, that's manipulative. To me, it's eye-opening.

"My brother gave up his career to look out for mine. When I came to New York because my parents were sick of supporting me, he let me move in. I just don't think that kind of man should have to suffer for the one selfish thing he finally did for himself."

Lilah felt incredibly foolish. "I—I didn't say— I mean, I just don't think he and I are—"

"I'm not here to beg you to take him back. He's absolutely miserable over this. But if you don't love my brother, that's your right. If he's not what you're looking for, that's fine. But if you do love him, and if a hardworking upstanding kind of guy is what you're looking for, then the reason you two aren't together is *your choice*."

Lilah felt her cheeks stinging with embarrassment. This was as raw and exposed as she'd ever felt. In the back of her mind she knew she'd blown up because she was scared. Everyone—Tyler, Angie and now Reggie—had tried to tell her that she was overreacting. But now she was forced to face it.

She'd sabotaged things with Tyler because she didn't trust herself. She picked the wrong man once before and the divorce had devastated her. But in retrospect, she really should have seen that Chuck wasn't right for her. He'd been a square peg that she'd been trying to cram into a round hole.

But with Tyler, things had been amazingly simple. She'd gravitated to him like a fully charged magnet. They talked about serious issues, shared political views and laughed easily. Her relationship with Tyler was nothing like the one she had with Chuck.

Finally, Lilah looked up at Reggie. "Thanks for telling me all this. I'm not sure yet what to do with it. But you've done something kind and unselfish for your brother. You can feel good about that."

"Thanks, but not really."

"Why not?"

"Because he's hurting right now, and as usual, I'm about to abandon him."

"What do you mean?"

"I'm going to Atlanta for a while. I'm going to work with some people there, try to come up with a new sound. I'm leaving next week."

"Tyler's not going with you?"

"No. I essentially fired him. I told him he needs to be free of me and finally get back to living his dreams. He wished me well, but the truth is, I think he'll be pretty lost for a while, trying to figure out what to do now that he doesn't have to take care of me."

Lilah felt a weird prickling at the back of her neck, and she looked up and saw a trio of teenage girls gaping in through the window. They were watching Reggie eat. "I think your fans have found you. Do you ever get used to that?"

He waved and turned on his bright pearly smile. The three girls clapped and jumped up and down. "No, that's what it's all about," he said.

Chapter 25

Tyler froze in place as he watched his brother wave at three young and adoring fans through the restaurant window. He was with Lilah.

Rage and betrayal swarmed in him, and his body warred with whether or not to rush forward or hastily retreat. His legs on autopilot, Tyler found himself headed back toward the subway.

She wouldn't even speak to him, but she'd sit down and have a nice lunch—at his favorite café, no less—with Reggie.

Wasn't this just typical? His brother had no regard for his—

Suddenly, Tyler stopped cold in the middle of

the street. The honking of a cab rushing toward him brought him back to his senses. He leaped out of the street to safety before the cab could bear down on him.

What had he been thinking? That his brother was trying to start something with Lilah? That was absurd and he knew better. If they were having lunch, Reggie was there to plead his case.

After spending the entire day moping around his apartment, Tyler had decided he needed some air and a club sandwich. But seeing the two of them sitting in that window, laughing the way he used to laugh with her, had brought on a bout of temporary insanity.

What should he do now? Go back and find out first-hand if his brother's words had worked in his favor? No, he couldn't do that. It would look too much like a setup. Plus, he had little faith in Lilah changing her mind.

Maybe in a week or two, once she'd had time to mull things over, but if she was angry enough to shut him out so completely, she wasn't likely to reconsider things because of his brother.

Tyler felt his chest constricting. It was actually pretty cool of his brother to go down there to try to help him. He'd been leaning on him pretty heavily for the last day or so, and to his great surprise, Reggie had been a solid support. He had a pretty rosy view of life and tried to impart that carefree spirit to Tyler.

But now, just as the two of them were starting to really get to know each other, the kid would be going away for a while. They'd spent so much of their lives right on top of each other. But it wasn't until Tyler had let his guard down and let his brother help him for a change that he really got to see the kind of man his brother had become.

And he respected the fact that Reggie had finally stood up to him, deciding it was time for him to go out into the world on his own. Tyler regretted all the time they spent at odds because he'd insisted on treating his brother like a child. But in the future, even though they may not be in close proximity, Tyler knew he and Reggie would be close friends.

Tyler kept walking past the subway station, just letting his legs propel him forward. It was Lilah's birthday today. He'd had many visions about how they would spend that day, but it had never occurred to him that he might not be a part of it.

She no longer wanted him there. He had to accept that. In his heart of hearts, he knew they would be together again eventually. He just had to give her time. He'd wait till she returned home, then in a week or two, maybe he'd take a trip out to D.C. He could stay with his parents for a while. That way, if she didn't come around right away, he could at least catch up with them and some old friends from high school.

After all, with Reggie leaving, he'd have a lot more free time on his hands. There were a few clients to wrap things up with, but it wouldn't take long to find them new representation. Over the years, it had gotten exhausting fending off competitors who wanted to steal his clients.

The more he walked and thought about his future, the more he liked the idea of moving back to D.C. Not just for a visit, but permanently. There were a lot of nonprofit organizations and lobbying groups in the Capital city. There was a lot of good work to be done.

Feeling empowered by his new resolve, Tyler quickened his step, deciding to walk the rest of the way home. The walk would take much longer, but he had a lot of plans to make.

He started a mental list. *1. Win Lilah back.*

When Lilah returned to her hotel, she couldn't stop thinking about the things Reggie had said. She felt like a fool. She was going to give up a chance at real love after just one argument? She'd given her husband chance after chance in a marriage that was doomed to fail.

And Tyler? What had she given him besides a guilt trip?

She was running away because she was afraid to trust her instincts. Had she learned nothing in the past two weeks?

A dawn of realization came over her. If she'd followed her instincts, she never would have married Chuck in the first place. He may have looked good on paper, but her heart had never been blind to his faults. She'd married him because she thought they would adjust. Lilah had hoped that if she worked hard enough at it, the relationship would thrive.

The problem wasn't that she couldn't trust her instincts. The problem was that she'd been ignoring them. And right now they were telling her that Tyler was the one.

Standing in the middle of the hotel Grande lobby, Lilah started dialing her cell phone. No answer at Tyler's apartment. She dialed his cell. No answer. After leaving messages at both numbers for him to meet her at the party, Lilah went back to her room.

Suddenly she was really looking forward to her birthday party.

"Okay, you can come out now," Angie called to Lilah, who had been sequestered in the bedroom.

Lilah walked into the living room and saw that the caterers had set up tables of food along the walls. An ice sculpture in the shape of a thirty sat in the middle of the main table.

"Wow, Angie. All of this looks amazing. You didn't have to get the ice sculpture. I thought we'd both agreed that I'd gotten a bit carried away with all of that."

"Some of it. I thought the ice sculpture was a good idea."

Angie turned on the stereo system and music began pouring from the speakers provided by the hotel. Twenty minutes later her first guests arrived, Maureen and her boyfriend.

"Hey, Lilah, I want to introduce you to Alex. I've been telling him all about you. And he's been reading your blog, too."

Lilah shook his hand and exchanged pleasantries with them. "Maureen, just how many people were you telling about my blog?" she asked after Alex left to check out the open bar.

The redhead blushed enough to match her hair. "It turned out to be a good conversation piece. Besides, the more, the better, right?"

"Right," Lilah said, laughing.

"So what's left? You haven't updated your blog in two days. Are you done?"

"No, and I'm probably not going to finish. It's already my birthday, you know."

"Actually, Angie told me you were born at 11:29 p.m. That still gives you four hours. Come on, where's The List? Let's see what's left."

It was pointless to argue, so Lilah gave in. "She showed Maureen her printout. "See, these last few things aren't likely to get done."

Maureen sighed. "Aw, Date Reggie Martin. You never got to that one."

Lilah paused. "Actually, this afternoon I had lunch with him."

Maureen's face lit up. "That counts." She dug in her purse, pulled out a pen and crossed it off The List. "Okay, what about *protest a worthy cause.* Maybe we can stage some kind of sit-in tonight."

"Oh, you won't have to do that. I actually took care of that one yesterday. I marched in a rally."

Maureen crossed it off The List. "See, now that you've got a momentum built up, The List is practically taking care of itself."

Lilah paused. That was true. She'd stopped actively pursuing The List shortly after she and Tyler got together. It started to feel less important to her. But The List items had continued to get completed. After she'd stopped trying to meet up with Reggie, he'd walked right into her life. She hadn't ever asked him for the date, but today he'd shown up and taken her to lunch.

Lilah looked back down at the paper in Maureen's hands. "There are still two unchecked items and those are both tall orders."

Maureen studied it. "Fifteen minutes of fame? Does blogging count? You must have thousands of hits on your site."

"I'm sorry, but I'm pretty sure that doesn't count."

"Well, maybe we can start a fire and get on the evening news."

"I don't think so."

"All right, let me see the other one. 'Drink Cristal champagne straight from the bottle.' All we have to do is order some from room service."

"Do you know how expensive that stuff is?" Lilah protested.

"This coming from the woman staying in a fancy place like this? I'm going to leave a job application downstairs because there's bound to be a pay upgrade to work here."

"You're right. I guess we can—"

Remy and Belle walked into the suite and swept Lilah up in a big hug. After Lilah had made introductions, Remy handed Lilah a narrow gift bag. "This is for you, Lilah. Happy birthday."

"And, child, if you don't feel like sharing it, you don't have to. That's one thing you learn as you get older. Keep the good stuff to yourself," Belle said.

Lilah reached into the bag and pulled out a bottle of Cristal champagne. Lilah and Maureen exchanged wide-eyed looks.

Maureen picked up her pen. "Check!"

After that it was a virtual who's who of not just her journey in New York, but her life in general. The party started filling up with some of her high

274   *Lilah's List*

school friends, several people she came in contact with in New York, including her favorite driver, Sanjay. And the funniest part of it all was that many of the guests were carrying copies of The List around and checking off items as they mingled with each other.

Lilah felt anxious when, two hours into the party, Tyler still hadn't shown up. "Maybe he's still angry and doesn't plan on coming," she said to Angie.

"That's just crazy. When he gets your message, he'll come. Maybe if you hadn't given him the cold shoulder for so long…"

"I know, you told me so, blah, blah, blah. I get it. I was wrong. All I can think about now is how to fix things with him. I'm going to try calling again."

Lilah slipped away into the bedroom and tried both of Tyler's numbers for the fifth time that day. Still no answer.

"I guess it serves me right," she said to herself as she hung up the phone. For the past two days she'd avoided him, and now she was getting a taste of her own medicine.

Worry clutched her heart. It just wasn't like Tyler to ignore her on purpose. If he hadn't returned her calls it was probably because he hadn't received her messages.

For all she knew he could be lying in a gutter

somewhere. Lilah sank down onto the bed in defeat.

Angie poked her head into the room. "Aren't you coming back out to the party?"

"I can't find Tyler, and I'm worried something's happened to him."

"Don't worry, I'm sure he's fine. Why don't you come out and talk to your guests? That will keep your mind off it."

Lilah let herself be dragged back to the party because she didn't want to be rude. But her heart just wasn't in it.

Tyler opened the door to his apartment that evening, and nearly jumped out of his skin when Reggie leaped off the couch. "Where have you been?"

"Man, you scared me half to death. What are you doing here?"

"Your phone's been ringing off the hook. Lilah's been trying to reach you."

"She has?"

"Yeah. Come on. I was headed to her party, and I stopped by here to get you. I've been listening to her leaving messages on your machine for the last two hours. Where were you?"

"I had some errands to run. Since you're going to Atlanta, I've decided to move back to D.C."

Reggie paused to soak that in for a second.

"Wow. Okay, we'll talk about that on the way. Come on, we should head over there now."

"You go on ahead. I need to shower first. Just tell her I'm on my way." Tyler paused. "I guess whatever you said to her must have worked."

Reggie stopped in his tracks. "You know about that?"

"Yeah, I saw you both through the window of the café."

"You were there? Why didn't you come in?"

"To be honest, at first, I was mad. But once I cooled down, I realized you were probably trying to help me."

"Damn right." Reggie grinned. "Honestly, bro? I don't know what you're going to do without me."

Tyler shook his head. "I don't know, either."

It was just after eleven, and Lilah had begun to lose hope of Tyler showing up when she saw Reggie walk into the suite. Her heart leaped and she started toward him. She hesitated when she saw a reporter and cameraman follow him into the room.

He motioned for them to wait before he crossed the room to talk to her. "They were in the lobby looking for a way into this party," he said, pointing to the camera crew. "They knew the date from your blog, and they'd checked out all the hotels looking for you."

Lilah gasped. "For me? You're kidding."

"No, apparently half the city's been following your adventures."

She was stunned. But it didn't matter. Only one thing mattered right now. "Where's Tyler?"

"He's coming. He was running around town all day, I'll let him tell you why, but he didn't get any of your messages. He wanted me to tell you he's on his way."

Lilah felt her body release with relief. "He's definitely coming? You talked to him?"

"Yes, I spoke to him. He loves you. And he's coming."

"He said that? He said he loves me?"

"No, I'm saying that. But it's true."

Lilah nodded, feeling in the mood to party for the first time all night. Looking past Reggie, she saw Angie talking with the camera crew. Before Lilah could process what she was seeing, Angie was pointing in her direction.

Next thing she knew, the reporter was shoving a microphone in her face and asking her questions.

"So you're the woman whose blog is taking New York City's underground by storm. I understand that this is your thirtieth birthday party, how far did you get on Lilah's List?"

Stunned, Lilah wanted to ask a few questions herself, like how they knew about her blog, and did they really think their viewers cared? But she knew there wasn't time for that.

"Pursuing The List has been an adventure and a learning process," she said to the reporter. "There were some things on The List that I didn't even want to do anymore, like getting a tattoo and riding a motorcycle, that proved to be some of my most enlightening experiences. Then there were things on The List that I thought I was done with long ago that I discovered were unfinished."

"Like what?" the reporter asked.

"Like fall in love. I crossed that off The List when I was twenty-two. Now, with—" she glanced down at her watch "—just about fifteen minutes before I officially turn thirty, I'm just realizing that I've fallen in love for real and for the first time."

"That's amazing. Who's the lucky man?"

Lilah smiled coyly. "With R&B singing sensation Reggie Martin's brother, Tyler."

"Let me get this straight. You're in love with *Tyler* Martin. Not Reggie. But wasn't 'date Reggie Martin' on your list?"

"That's right, but sometimes we can focus so hard on what we think we want, that we don't see what we really need is right in front of us."

Lilah finished the interview and the party resumed. She started looking around the room and saw Tyler coming toward her from the doorway.

"Tyler, I—"

"You don't have to say anything. I heard everything. I love you, too."

"But I want to apologize—"

"Shh." He bent down, picked Lilah up and swept her into his arms. "There's plenty of time for that once we have a little privacy."

Everyone at the party started whooping and cheering as Tyler headed for the bedroom door.

Through the noise Lilah heard Angie say to Maureen, "Okay, I think that officially makes this a wild party."

Maureen giggled. "Check!"

Epilogue

Lilah's List Blog Entry
October 27, 2009

I eloped last night. That's right, Tyler and I decided to forgo all the fanfare and just do it. We were having trouble finding the time to plan a big wedding with Tyler's advocacy group, People for Change, just getting off the ground, and me writing my new column, "Lilah's List," for the *Washington Post*. Besides, with Reggie starting his world tour next month—I hope you've all bought your copies of his new album *Heat*—and Angie pursuing fashion inspiration in Paris, it was just easier. And before you ask. No, I'm not pregnant. But it is item number two on the new list.

Lilah's New List

1. ~~Marry Tyler Martin~~
2. Have a baby
3. Live happily ever after

*A dramatic new novel about learning
to trust again…*

Essence bestselling author

ANITA BUNKLEY

SUITE
Embrace

Too many Mr. Wrongs has made Skylar Webster gun-shy.
But seductive Olympic athlete Mark Jorgen is awfully
tempting. Mark's tempted, too, enough to consider
changing his globe-trotting, playboy ways. But first he'll
have to earn Skylar's trust.

"Anita Bunkley has a gift for bringing wonderful ethnic
characters and their unique problems to readers in a
dramatic, sweeping novel of tragedy and triumph."
—*Romantic Times BOOKreviews* on *Wild Embers*

Coming the first week of January wherever books are sold.

KIMANI™
ROMANCE

www.kimanipress.com   KPAB0480108

The sensual sequel to
THE GLASS SLIPPER PROJECT...

Taming MARIELLA

Bestselling Arabesque author
DARA GIRARD

Model-turned-photographer Mariella Duvall and
troubleshooter Ian Cooper butt heads on Mariella's new
project—until they're stranded together in the middle of
nowhere. Suddenly, things heat up in a very pleasurable way.
But what will happen when they return to reality?

"A true fairy tale...Dara Girard's *The Glass Slipper Project*
is a captivating story."
—*Romantic Times BOOKreviews* (4 stars)

Coming the first week of January wherever books are sold.

A deliciously sensual tale of passion and revenge...

Sweeter Than Revenge

Bestselling author

Ann
CHRISTOPHER

When daddy cuts her off, Maria must take a position as
executive assistant to David Hunt—a man who once broke
her heart. But David's back in her life for only one reason—
revenge! And he knows the sweetest way to get it....

"Just About Sex is an exceptional story!"
—*Romantic Times BOOKreviews* (4-1/2 stars)

Coming the first week of January wherever books are sold.

KIMANI™
ROMANCE

Even a once-in-a-lifetime love
deserves a second chance.

USA TODAY Bestselling Author

BRENDA
JACKSON

WHISPERED PROMISES

A Madaris Family novel.

When Caitlin Parker is called to her father's deathbed,
she's shocked to find her ex-husband, Dex Madaris,
there, as well. It's been four years since Caitlin and Dex
said goodbye, shattering the promise of an everlasting
love that never was. But the true motive for their
unexpected reunion soon comes to light, as does the
daughter Dex never knew existed—a secret Caitlin
fears Dex will never forgive....

"Brenda Jackson has written another sensational novel...
stormy, sensual and sexy—all the things a romance reader
could want in a love story."
—*Romantic Times BOOKreviews* on *Whispered Promises*

Available the first week of January
wherever books are sold.

ARABESQUE®

www.kimanipress.com

KPBJ0510108

*Can love work enough magic to make
three people's wishes come true?*

Award-winning author

Janice Sims

Three Wishes

Adopted at birth, attorney Sunny Adams learns that
Hollywood actress Audra Kane is her real mother.
Though she longs to visit her in L.A., she won't abandon
the murder case she's working on—not even when Audra's
gorgeous stepson Jonas Blake is the one who's asking.

Sunny is the most beautiful, strong-willed woman
Jonas ever met, and he's happy to stay and protect her
until her dangerous case is over. Getting involved with
Sunny gives him hope that he can make her a permanent
part of his own life....

*Available the first week of January
wherever books are sold.*

ARABESQUE®

www.kimanipress.com

KPJS0110108

Featuring the voices of eighteen of your
favorite authors...

ON THE LINE

Essence Bestselling Author
donna hill

A sexy, irresistible story starring Joy Newhouse,
who, as a radio relationship expert, is considered
the diva of the airwaves. But when she's fired,
Joy quickly discovers that if she can dish it out,
she'd better be able to take it!

Featuring contributions by such favorite authors
as Gwynne Forster, Monica Jackson, Earl Sewell,
Phillip Thomas Duck and more!

Coming the first week of January,
wherever books are sold.

sepia™

www.kimanipress.com   KPDH0211207